I went to the door of the bathroom on the hall and felt my feet becoming rooted to the floor.

Right beside me, Jill made a strangled sound.

It was a luxurious bath, done in pale green tile, with lots of mirrors. Sam had set out a shaving kit, which had been emptied into the bathtub; shaving cream had been sprayed out across the surrounding tile. Toothbrushes and toothpaste had been dumped together in the sink, and there was a red smear on the edge of the vanity that sent prickles racing over my bare skin.

Jill found her voice before I found mine. "Is it . . . blood . . . ?"

Also by Willo Davis Roberts
Published by Fawcett Juniper Books:

BABY-SITTING IS A DANGEROUS JOB

DARK SECRETS

Willo Davis Roberts

FAWCETT JUNIPER • NEW YORK

1

It was almost dark when we finally got to Allendale, and when I saw where we were going to spend the first month of my ruined vacation, I couldn't believe it.

The final week of school had been the most humiliating and disappointing period of my entire life, and if I hadn't wanted so badly to get out of Granite Falls where I didn't have to face anybody I knew, I'd never have let Sam talk me into joining him on his new job. And now it was obvious he'd misrepresented this "estate" where I was stuck for the next four weeks.

My little brother Mickey said part of what I was thinking when the station wagon pulled up in front of the low log and stone building.

"Wow! Spooky! Is this place haunted or something?"

He had a point. In the dusk the cottage where we would be staying almost disappeared in the thick cedars and firs, and the overall impression was one of abandonment. The station wagon rolled to a stop and Sam turned off the ignition.

"No, it's just been empty for over a year, and nobody's taken care of it."

"That's for sure. The grass is a foot deep."

We could see that nobody'd done any mowing or pruning for a long time. The trees pressed in around the cottage, and we couldn't even see the main house Sam was going to be caretaker for. I felt overwhelmed with the certainty that it wasn't going to be any better than this.

Beside me in the backseat, Jill stirred. Uneasily, I thought. More humiliation coming my way, I supposed. I hardly knew her, because she'd only moved to Granite a few weeks earlier, but she was pretty and blond and seemed nice enough. I'd invited her on impulse, and on the thirty-mile ride from home I'd already begun to regret it. She'd hardly said a word—so much for the company I wanted—and now, after I'd told her about this place that belonged to a rich family, where we were going to have such a great time—well, I was sure she was no more impressed than I was. I could have strangled Sam for building it up to me, and I'd been stupid enough to repeat what he said to *her*.

Tears of frustration stung my eyes, but I blinked them away. I'd done all the crying I was going to do, I thought, and clenched my teeth for a minute before I spoke in an almost normal voice.

"Well," I said, "this is it. Everybody out. Where's the key, Sam? Open the door and let us in, and I'll dig out the hot dogs. They're about the fastest thing to fix."

Jill took the cluster of keys Sam thrust at her as she stepped out of the car. "Unlock it, and we'll be along with the gear, right behind you," he said.

The interior light came on when Sam opened his door, and I saw that Jill's cheeks were pink. She turned color every time he looked at her or spoke to her.

Oh, this was going to be a fun summer. I wished I could walk away from my brothers, this girl I hardly knew, and all the kids I'd known all my life and now hated. Only I couldn't go anywhere else, and there were no other people out here in the sticks, so I couldn't even hope to meet a new friend.

I slid off the seat, knowing there wasn't much I could do except make the best of it.

A mosquito buzzed my cheek and I swatted at it, following

Jill toward the cottage. I would *not* cry, I would not be rude to Jill—after all, it wasn't her fault my life was a total mess—and I wouldn't leave myself open to any more of Sam's cutting comments by revealing how sorry I was feeling for myself, even though I had plenty of reason for it.

I'd expected better from Sam than I'd had through this crisis, I thought as Sam began hauling stuff out of the back of the station wagon. Sam was nineteen, five years older than I was, and he'd usually been pretty supportive, but his reaction to the events of the past couple of weeks had hurt almost as much as everything else that had gone before.

There were frogs croaking somewhere in the distance. Somehow that made it seem very lonely. I wished Mickey hadn't made that remark about the place being haunted.

"Mick, you take the sleeping bags in," Sam ordered. "They're about the only things that aren't breakable. Lisa, first order of things is food."

"Isn't it always," I said, resigned. "I knew you brought me just to cook."

"And to wash dishes," he confirmed, grinning. "I have to study, you know."

"I thought you were supposed to be working here," Mickey said, accepting the first of the sleeping bags.

"Caretaking. Not much work involved in that." Sam grabbed a box of groceries. "Just keep vandals from breaking windows, that kind of thing."

Jill had the door open by the time I got there. "I haven't found the light switch yet," she said, her face a pale oval in the dimness of the cottage.

"Try behind the door," Sam suggested. "It's an old place. They did things funny in those days. Mick, the bedrooms are over this way. That's the kitchen."

"Whew! It stinks in here!" Mickey said, turning from the doorway on the right.

3

He was right about that. I hesitated with my box of groceries.

"Dead mice," Jill said unexpectedly, and groped around on the wall just ahead of me. "There, I found that switch, now maybe I can find one for the living room."

The overhead bulb wasn't very big, but for a moment the brilliance made me blink. I lowered the box onto the counter and then yipped.

"You're right about the dead mouse. There it is." It had a sickening half-sweet, half-rotten odor that made me hold my breath.

It was lying in the sink. I wondered uneasily if there were more dead mice—or live ones—in other places. "Sam!"

"I'll get rid of it," Jill said, and a moment later she carried the smelly creature out the back door on a dustpan and flung it into the bushes.

Sam stuck his head in from the living room. "Supper ready yet?"

I gave him a dirty look and began to unload the box. I sure wasn't going to worry about fixing a four-course meal tonight, I decided. We'd gotten such a late start, what with waiting for Mom and Dad to leave for the airport on their trip to Brussels, then waiting some more for that dippy Mrs. Gottman, who was going to house-sit with the plants and the cat. It had been suppertime before we even left home, but Sam said we couldn't eat until we got here, so everybody was starving. It wouldn't matter, for one night, if the meal was nutritious or not.

I found the hot dogs and dumped them in a pan of water to heat on the old-fashioned stove, then rummaged for catsup, relish, and mustard. Sam liked onions on his, too, but I decided coldly that it wouldn't hurt him to do without for once.

He came in with the last load, sounding as if we were all here to have a great time. "Not bad, is it?"

4

I didn't answer, rolling my eyes at Jill. I'd never been to her house, so I didn't know what it was like, but it had to be better than this.

Jill, however, didn't react at all. I began to hope, rather desperately, that she wasn't going to stay mute and pink the entire month we'd be stuck here, until Mom and Dad came back from Europe.

"Whew!" Sam said. "Let's open some windows and get the smell of that mouse out of here."

Either the fresh air worked, or we got used to the odor, though when I took my first bite I felt a bit queasy. We ate most of the hot dogs and a package of cookies before we explored the rest of the place. That didn't take long.

The kitchen itself was old-fashioned, with a range and a refrigerator that looked like they should have been displayed in a museum. "You knew it didn't have a dishwasher," I accused Sam as I ran hot water into the sink and left the dishes to soak clean. "Why didn't you mention it so Mom could have got us some paper plates?"

"Oh," Sam said amiably, "did I mention that Beau's expecting some of your world-famous burritos when he comes?"

I stopped so suddenly that he ran into me in the doorway to the living room. "Beau's coming? And you expect me to cook for him?"

Beau was his college roommate at the U. Dub, which is what they call the University of Washington in Seattle. Sam would be a sophomore there next year if he studied enough this summer to make up what he'd missed out on because of an emergency appendectomy two months ago, and so was Beau. I'd never met him, but I'd sure heard a lot about him. Beau was the epitome of everything Sam thought *he* wasn't: suave, good-looking, popular, and rich.

"He's just a guy," Sam said now, shoving me ahead of him into the adjoining room, where we'd finally located the

5

light switches, behind the door. "Of course, he's kind of girl crazy. Beau always has three or four girls hanging around. And he likes to eat. I bragged about your cooking."

I jabbed him in the ribs with an elbow. "What else have you managed to forget to tell me that you've let me in for?" I wasn't quite joking. Beau would at least be a new person to meet; he might keep this month from being a total loss. Only I wasn't likely to impress him with my cooking unless he was a freak for Mexican food.

"Nothing," Sam assured me. "See, this is going to be pretty comfortable, don't you think?"

This was kind of old-fashioned, too, but in a living room it didn't matter as much. It was fairly good-sized, cedar-paneled, and there was a stone fireplace and easy chairs and a long sofa with a faded slipcover.

"Can we use the fireplace, if it gets cool enough?" Mickey wanted to know.

"Sure. There's dry wood stacked out back. The girls can pick which bedroom they want, I'll take the other one, and you, my young friend, can sleep on the screened porch at the back. Lisa, there's only one bathroom, so there'll be a five-minute time limit allowed in there at rush hour, okay?"

I didn't bother to respond. I was still thinking about his friend Beau. I wouldn't mind meeting a great-looking guy, even if he probably would think a fourteen-year-old was an infant, but I couldn't help being a little bit suspicious of a boy whose advance billing was so overpowering. There must be *something* less than perfect about Beau.

Sam hadn't waited for us to choose our room. "You take that one, I'll take this one, okay?"

I peered through the doorway of first one bedroom, then the other. Not much to choose between them except that the one he'd chosen had a double bed, the other one twin beds.

If it had been Marcia here with me, instead of Jill, who was almost a stranger, I'd have taken the double bed. I didn't

6

want to think about Marcia, who had been my best friend for as long as I could remember and was now my enemy.

"Okay," I agreed. "Mickey, this isn't my sleeping bag. Trade back."

"What's the difference?" Mickey asked. He had a way of looking innocent, with his round, freckled face and greenish eyes like mine, but he made one mistake. Whenever he held his eyes so wide open—so charmingly, so convincingly—we knew he was up to something.

"The difference," I said, handing over his own sleeping bag, "is that you slept in yours with the dog at Stinson's and it's probably full of fleas. Trade."

I turned to inspect the bathroom. That took even less time, since it was about the size of a small closet. Shower, no tub. And it looked as if it could stand scrubbing before we used it. It wasn't filthy, just long unused.

Like Scarlett O'Hara, I'd worry about it tomorrow.

"You said there's a swimming pool at the main house," I said, moving out of the doorway so Jill could see into the bathroom. I hoped she wasn't put off by the less-than-classy surroundings she'd been invited to share. "Is there water in it so we can use it?"

"Sure. It's got a cover over it to keep dirt and leaves out, so all we have to do is roll it off. We can walk up in the morning and look it over."

"Can we look in the house, too? I've never seen a mansion before, have you, Jill?" Since she was just following along behind us, saying nothing, I tried to draw her into the conversation.

Jill, however, only shook her head. I couldn't tell from her face what she thought of the caretaker's cottage. She was probably trying to make the best of things, too.

"Mick," Sam said, "what did you do with the flashlight? I think I'll walk up to the house tonight, just to make sure everything's all right."

"Can I go?" Mickey wanted to know.

"Why not? You can protect me from the spooks," Sam joked as they went out the door.

The lights were on all over the cottage now, and it wasn't spooky, just quietly dusty and looking as if no one had lived there for a long time. So I don't know why I jumped the way I did when the phone rang.

Who on earth knew we were here? Mom and Dad had only left that day, and I wasn't sure they'd have even reached New York yet on their way to Europe. Sam had had the phone reconnected, but he hadn't known the number, so he couldn't have given it to them, anyway. The same went for Mrs. Gottmann, at our house.

It rang four times before I located it, on one shelf of a bookcase beside the fireplace.

"Hello?" I said.

Nobody answered. "Hello?" I said again. "Who's this?"

There was still no answer, though this time I was sure I could hear breathing at the other end of the line.

"Who are you calling?" I demanded.

After a few more seconds of breathing, there was a click and the return of the dial tone.

"Wrong number?" Jill asked as I hung up.

"Yeah, I guess so." Yet for some reason it made me uneasy. If the caller had simply dialed a wrong number, why hadn't they said so? Why all those long moments of breathing in my ear? "Kids fooling around, maybe. Dialing at random or something."

Jill nodded. "This is kind of a nice place, isn't it?"

Nice? That was startling. On the other hand, though it wasn't fancy, it wasn't awful, either. "There're some games here. Let's see if there's anything worth playing," I suggested. "I warn you, though, Sam always wins word games like Scrabble. I suppose Pictionary is too new to be here. Hmm. You like Monopoly?"

Jill moistened her lips and spoke hesitantly. "I haven't played in a long time. Not since . . . my mother died."

"Oh, gosh, I'm sorry. I didn't know." I felt awkward, uncertain what to say. "Was it . . . did it happen recently?"

"A little over a year ago," Jill said very softly.

I didn't want to talk about it but didn't quite know how to change the subject. My mom says people who are grieving sometimes need more than anything else to talk about the person they've lost, so I tried.

"It . . . must be very hard to lose your mother," I said.

"Yes," Jill agreed. She didn't look at me but was inspecting the boxes of games on the shelf in front of us.

"There's only you and your dad left, then?" Why didn't Sam come back, I thought wildly, and get me out of this?

"That's right. Only the two of us." She cleared her throat. "I have grandparents—my mother's folks. I wonder if all the playing pieces are here for this one?"

I didn't even notice which game she chose. All I cared about was that she stop talking about her mother dying.

When Sam and Mickey came back we never did get around to playing the game. Mickey discovered there were some old 78s in a record cabinet, and we played them, listening mostly to comedy routines from years ago.

"I wonder who lived here," I said.

"Hired help," Sam guessed. "Same as now. This was the ideal job for me, with all the studying I have to do. It won't take much of my time, making rounds a couple of times a day and making sure no one who's unauthorized comes on the property."

"What're you going to do if they do?" Mickey wanted to know. "Shoot 'em?"

"Sure." Sam cocked a finger and pointed it at him. "Bank, bang. No, twirp, I'll just tell them it's private property and to get lost. Hey, did we bring any popcorn?"

We had, and guess who got to pop it?

By the time we finished eating that, we were all tired enough to go to bed.

We had decided ahead of time not to bring sheets and stuff. I knew who'd get stuck with making up beds and doing the laundry. So all we had to do was spread out sleeping bags on the beds and leave them open because it was warm.

I put on my pajamas and turned to see Jill buttoning up hers, a pair of fancy pale blue ones with lace and embroidery. I felt drab in my plain yellow ones.

"Pretty," I said, and for some reason even that made her blush.

"I hope you pick somebody different from Marcia for your next best friend," Sam had told me after the big smasheroo when I'd screamed at her for being too cowardly to tell the truth about the stolen test answer sheet.

Well, Jill wasn't much like Marcia, that was for sure. Jill was not a leader, was not pushy, was not, I was beginning to think, especially interesting.

On the other hand, she had taken the mouse out of the sink and disposed of it.

I decided not to make up my mind about Jill until more of the facts were in.

After I turned out the light I couldn't seem to go to sleep right away. If Marcia had been there—before she turned creep and sacrificed me for her own hide—we'd have talked and giggled until we got sleepy. Jill didn't say anything except good night, so I was left with my own thoughts.

I had planned such a great summer. This was probably better than sitting at home watching Marcia come and go with a new set of friends, right across the street from me, I rationalized. At least everybody in town wouldn't know I was left out of all the fun.

I was finally dozing off when I felt the weight of my little brother's body on the edge of the bed, at the same time that he said, "Lisa, wake up!"

I blinked, opening my eyes to darkness. "What's the matter?"

"There's a bear or something outside," Mickey said. "Can bears claw their way through screens?"

I rose on one elbow. "Mick, there aren't any bears around here."

"There's something," Mickey insisted. "I heard it crashing through the bushes at the back of the house."

"Come on, give me a break. I'm trying to sleep. There's nothing out there."

His voice trembled. "I heard it. The bushes crackled and I said, 'Go away,' and it stopped. And then it started again. Something *big*, Lisa, honest."

He was really scared. I couldn't ignore that. I sighed. "Okay. Let's get the flashlight and look."

"I brought it with me, but I was afraid to turn it on," he confessed, handing it over.

In the other bed Jill slept on her side, blond hair falling forward over her face. We moved quietly past Sam's door, but he heard us anyway.

"What's going on?" he asked drowsily.

"Mickey thinks there's a bear in the bushes outside. Listen, Mick, instead of running around when we can't see anything, why don't we just bring your sleeping bag into Sam's room? All right, Sam?"

"Sure," Sam muttered, already falling back to sleep.

While we were on the screened porch I aimed the flashlight out into the woods behind the house, but there was nothing to see except trees.

I got Mickey settled on the floor in Sam's room and crawled back into bed.

Sometime later I woke, groggy and disoriented, to a peculiar and ominous sound.

I was reluctant to wake up; I was too tired. This didn't feel like my own bed. Where was I?

Then I remembered and opened my eyes, because I'd also remembered Mickey's fear of the bear. It wasn't a bear that threatened us, though.

There was a flickering light visible through the open doorway into the hall. I knew then what the alarming sound was: crackling flames. And I could smell the smoke.

2

For a few seconds I was paralyzed with fear. Then I scrambled out of the sleeping bag, stumbling against Jill's bed as I yelled.

"Sam! Wake up! The house is on fire!"

I heard Jill make a kind of choked sound, so I knew she was awake. I ran toward the living room.

Flames raced up the draperies, scorching the cedar walls, licking at the ceiling. Luckily the phone was on my side of the room, and even though I'd never been so scared in my life, I managed to dial 911.

The voice of the emergency operator was calm, but when a strip of burning fabric fell from the window across a chair, I screamed for help. Jill ran past me and grabbed a throw rug to beat at the chair that had begun to smolder.

I had no idea what the address was here, and I panicked, but the operator's voice forced me out of the numbness. "The gatehouse, at Allendale, on . . . Sam! Where is this place?"

"The Allendale place? On Malcolm Road? We'll have a crew there in a few minutes. And ma'am, get out of the house. Do you understand?"

"Yes," I said, and dropped the phone. "Get out of the house!" I yelled.

Jill hesitated, because Sam was there in red shorts with a bucket he'd found somewhere. He threw water on the burning chair, and part of the fire went out, leaving an ugly black

13

a pan of water, Jill ran ... ... containers, until Sam yelled out

"Lisa's right! Get out of here! Now!"

We ran for our lives.

By the time the fire trucks arrived, the entire front of the cottage was involved. It was a terrible feeling to watch it go. Yet we retreated no farther than we had to, to be safe.

We could feel the heat from a considerable distance away. Mickey's freckles stood out sharply on his round face, tinted pink by the flickering light. "My sleeping bag's in there," he said.

Sam rested a hand on his shoulder, holding him still as we stood on the drive, watching the menacing orange flames engulf the interior of the cottage. I felt so scared and helpless.

Actually, though, the fire fighters had the fire under control very quickly. There was an acrid smell that nearly turned my stomach, and I was shaking. So was Jill, and there were black smudges on her pretty pajamas. When I looked down, there were a couple of small black holes on my own, though I didn't have any burns as far as I could tell.

A man who introduced himself as the fire chief asked us questions about how it started, but we didn't know any more than he did. No, we hadn't had a fire in the fireplace, and none of us smoked.

"Well, we'll leave a couple of men here to make sure it's under control, and when it's daylight we'll have a look, see if we can tell how it started. I don't think you're going to want to spend the rest of the night here. Besides the smell, there may be fumes, and we put a lot of water in there. It's pretty much of a mess."

"I guess we better move up to the big house," Sam decided. "Is it okay if we go inside and get our clothes, and the keys?"

Subdued and still shaking, I helped carry out sleeping bags that were undamaged but had an unpleasant smoky smell and gather up our clothes to load in the station wagon. The kitchen was damaged and we knew we wouldn't be able to come back here to stay, so we silently loaded up our groceries, too.

Any other time I'd have been eager to see the big house. Now, in the dark and wondering if I'd even be able to sleep without nightmares, I couldn't work up much interest.

All I could tell was that the house they called Allendale, after the family that had lived in it for many years, was huge. Two stories high, with white pillars holding up the roof of the veranda across the front.

When Sam turned on the lights in the entrance hall, a magnificent crystal chandelier sparkled above us, and I felt only relief that the electricity had been left on.

Mickey looked around uneasily. "We're not gonna split up, are we?"

"No," Sam agreed immediately. "Let's spread our sleeping bags right here. We can choose rooms tomorrow."

So for the second time that night we went to bed, with boxes of food and our suitcases sitting around us, but we didn't sleep much.

I could tell by the breathing around me that the others weren't resting any better than I was. Even Mickey kept stirring restlessly in his sleeping bag.

For a while I didn't close my eyes, but stared upward in the dark. I must have relived waking up and finding the fire half a dozen times before I could let it go. Tired though I was, I couldn't relax.

I thought about Mom and Dad, winging their way across the Atlantic, out of reach. I thought about arriving at the cottage, and the awful smell that Jill had recognized at once as being a dead mouse. The rest of us had never smelled one, and I wondered how come *she* knew about dead mice.

It had cooled off now. I was shivering, so I closed my

sleeping bag. The trouble with that was that now the top flap was under my chin, and I kept on smelling the smoke.

Sleep, I told myself, but it didn't work.

I thought about Mickey waking me up the first time, thinking there was a bear outside. Boy, what a night!

A bear, and a fire, and a telephone that rang and there was nobody on the other end of the line . . . well, yes, someone had been there, someone who breathed audibly but didn't speak.

Each of those things, taken by itself, could have been dismissed without too much thought, if the fire was accidental.

Marcia—in the days when we were friends—used to say I let my imagination run away with me. It was sure doing it tonight.

What if it hadn't been a bear Mickey heard, but someone prowling around outside? Someone, maybe, who waited until we were all asleep, then started a fire that might have killed us all?

Even the phone call . . . to a number we hadn't given to anyone . . . took on a sinister significance as I lay there thinking about it.

A few yards away Sam rolled over with a thump, and I whispered his name.

"Yeah?" he muttered. "If I'd known we'd have to put our bags on the floor, I'd have brought air mattresses, too."

"Sam, did you leave the windows open when we went to bed? In the living room?"

"Sure. It was too warm to close them, and they were screened. Why?"

"It seemed as if the fire started by those front windows. I mean, it was the curtains I saw burning."

"The firemen'll figure it out, how it started." Sam grunted. "Go to sleep."

Easier said than done, I thought. *We* hadn't been careless with fire, hadn't even *had* a fire. So how had it started?

16

For the first time it occurred to me that maybe Sam had been hired as caretaker because vandals had caused problems before. Such as setting fires, maybe? "Sam," I ventured again, very softly, but he gave an exaggerated snore. He wasn't going to talk to me.

I didn't think I'd ever sleep again—at least not at Allendale—but I must have, because I dreamed. In the dream a dark, faceless form stalked me through the woods, silhouetted against the burning cottage.

I woke up, gasping, to find Mickey squatting beside me.

"What's the matter?" I was already looking around for the fire.

It was broad daylight, though, and except that I was in unfamiliar surroundings nothing appeared to be wrong.

"I'm hungry, and nobody else woke up," Mickey said.

Beyond him, Jill opened her eyes, and there were deep shadows beneath them, lavender smudges that showed plainly on her fair skin.

"Wow," I said, "I'll bet you're glad I invited you along with us."

She managed a faint grin. "It's been more exciting than I figured on," she admitted.

Sam's hair, standing on end, poked out above his sleeping bag. "Breakfast ready yet?" he asked, yawning.

I sat up and threw my pillow at him. "You guys turn your backs so we can get dressed, and then we'll go see if we can find the kitchen while you get up. Bring the boxes with you."

It was a better kitchen, when we located it, than the one at the caretaker's cottage. Dishwasher, I noted with as much satisfaction as I could manage after last night. Modern electric range, microwave, huge refrigerator/freezer.

"Scrambled eggs and toast," I decided when Mickey came in carrying the first of the boxes. "I suppose the orange juice is lukewarm; we should have put that stuff away last night."

Jill unloaded the boxes while I fixed breakfast. We were

17

kind of a scruffy-looking bunch as we sat around the Formica-topped table; we'd just grabbed whatever came to hand first, which for all four of us meant old jeans and T-shirts. Nobody but Jill had found socks so far.

Sam ate his last bite of toast with a big dollop of jam on it and wiped his mouth on a paper napkin. "Well, I guess I better go see if they've found out anything down at the cottage. I don't look forward to reporting that we had a fire the first night I'm on the job."

"Have they had trouble before?" I demanded. "Fires? Break-ins?"

"Not that I know of. They didn't mention it, just said they wanted me to keep vandals away. I thought they meant kids from town, out prowling around because they knew the place was empty." He hesitated before depositing his dishes on the edge of the sink. "I hope they've found some simple explanation for the fire. I'd hate to think anybody actually set it, just for the fun of it."

"Especially since they couldn't help seeing the place was occupied," I agreed. 'With the car sitting right in front of it."

Somehow that seemed less likely in daylight than it had in the middle of the night. "Wait a minute while we load the dishwasher, and we'll go with you," I said.

The firemen were gone, so we didn't find out what they thought about the origin of the fire. The scene was perfectly peaceful in the morning sunshine, if you didn't notice the smoke and fire damage around the windows.

Sam stood just inside the living room and looked around. "No way we're going to be able to move back in here."

"I hope they don't fire you because of this," I said uneasily, though in a way I wondered if we wouldn't be better off to pack up and go home.

"If they do, they do," Sam said flatly, but I knew he

dreaded having to report to the Allendales what had happened.

While he poked around inside, I examined the windows where I'd first seen the fire. They were open, all right, and the screens were on the ground, one of them looking as if someone had stepped through it.

Had the firemen removed the screen, or had someone else done it before they got there?

Mom and Dad would never have let us come if they'd suspected anything like this would happen. I knew what they'd tell us to do if they knew.

Mickey popped up behind me. "Something heavy was in the bushes where I heard the bear last night. The branches are all broken."

I followed him around the corner of the cottage, Jill trailing us. "The firemen broke them while they were here," I suggested, not wanting to give in again to my dark thoughts from the middle of the night.

Mickey suddenly knelt down and pushed aside some low-hanging branches. "See, there's footprints. Not a bear, though."

I squatted beside him. "Boots. I'm sure I saw the same tread out front. It was the firemen, Mick."

Mickey moved farther into the shrubbery, widening the exposure of damp earth where water directed onto the roof had drained off the back of the house. "What about this one? It doesn't have any tread, and it's smaller."

There was only part of a print, the heel section of it obliterated when a fireman had stepped on an earlier indentation. A shoe, not a boot.

My mouth was suddenly dry. I remembered clearly what it had been like, last night, watching the fire, the men who'd come on the yellow trucks. I was almost positive all the fire fighters had worn rubber boots.

I tried to sound offhand. "It's hard to tell. They're investigating, Mick. Come on, let's see if Sam's decided what we're going to do now.''

A part of me wished Sam would give up on this caretaking job and take us all home. Even having Mrs. Gottman fluttering around us wouldn't be any worse than waking up to find the house on fire.

"We can't go home," Sam decided when I asked him. "Beau's coming here when he gets back from his folks' in Boston. I gave him a map to find us, and I've got to wait for him. I'll call Mr. Allendale in Seattle and tell him what happened. Unless he fires me, we'll just move into the big house. Why don't you girls pick out the rooms you want. You too, Mick, while I take a general look around.''

It seemed so peaceful as we walked back toward the big house. It was really a beautiful place, I thought; at least it would be if the grass were cut and the weeds pulled up from the flower beds. The house was elegant, the grounds were spacious, and there was that lovely pool.

I could almost let myself believe there was nothing ominous about the things that had happened since we'd arrived here last night.

Almost.

3

I don't know if I would have been very much interested in the house if it hadn't been for Jill. She was fascinated by it.

"It's so beautiful," she said. "Look at that chandelier!"

I looked. There were hundreds of crystal prisms, and even though it hadn't been cleaned in a long time, they still sparkled. It *was* lovely.

"Let's see what's in here," Jill said, leading the way into one of the rooms off the main entryway. So I followed, and gradually I got interested, too. I'd never been in this kind of house before, a house that belonged to rich people. It looked like they'd enjoyed living here, because in spite of all the expensive furnishings, it had a homey feeling once we lifted the dustcovers on things.

"Oh, look, a library!" She paused in the doorway with a delighted smile. "I always wanted a library of my own, didn't you?" She didn't wait for a reply. "I saw pictures of a Tudor mansion in England that was like this, wood paneling and leaded-glass doors on the bookcases, and deep red carpeting. What'll you bet the furniture is real leather?"

She reached over to lift one of the covers from the nearest chair. "See! What did I tell you." She laughed ruefully. "Dad and I have moved around a lot since Mom died. We usually lived in rented rooms. Some of them didn't amount to much. I used to dream about places like this."

It was about as personal as anything she'd ever said to me,

21

except for telling me that her mom had died. I wondered how long it had been since she'd had anybody to talk to, like a close friend.

"It must be hard, moving around often, not having a real home of your own," I said awkwardly. I didn't actually know, because all my life I'd lived in Granite Falls in the same house I lived in now. Why should that suddenly make me feel guilty?

And then, for just a moment, I thought she was going to cry. When she spoke, though, her voice was flat. I must have imagined it.

"Yes." She turned away so I couldn't see her face. "Look, here's a humidor of tobacco and a pipe. My grandfather had one like it."

"Do your grandparents live around here?" I asked. There was something almost eerie about the way she stroked the surface of the table where the humidor and the pipe were displayed, leaving marks in the dust. I had the sudden horrid thought that maybe her grandfather was dead, too, and now she'd have to talk about *that*.

I had known everything about Marcia and she'd known everything about me. There hadn't been any of these difficult silences, the questions that turned out to be embarrassing or painful. For a few seconds I was swamped with regret, and then the anger took over again. How could a genuine friend have thrown suspicion on me, when she was the guilty one?

I was trying to turn the conversation away from her family when Jill finally said, "My grandparents live in Tacoma. Not so far away, but . . . Daddy doesn't get along with them very well. We tried living there for a few months after Mom died, and it . . . didn't work out. His own parents are dead, and there's nobody else. Relatives, I mean."

No relatives except grandparents you didn't get along with? It was an appalling idea. We have dozens of aunts and uncles and cousins on both sides of the family, plus two sets of grandparents, and we all had a great time whenever we got together. I didn't know how to talk to a girl like Jill, and I had to change the subject, fast.

"I've dreamed about fancy houses, too," I said, trying to get into the spirit of admiring the place. "I imagine myself in a pale green dress with a hoop skirt, coming down that curving stairway to meet a handsome man who's going to take me to a ball. You know, something with more class than a sock hop. I went to a couple of *those* last year with Rod Miller, but he's not my boyfriend or anything. My folks think fourteen is too early to have a boyfriend."

Jill was still moving around the room, touching things almost reverently. "I've never been anywhere with a boy. I haven't lived in one place long enough to . . . make friends. At least I guess that's what's happened. I'd hate to think I'll never make friends."

"As pretty as you are," I said bluntly, "the guys will be flocking around you when school starts next fall. A lot of them were looking at you the last few weeks."

I hoped that would make her feel better, but she was biting her lip.

"Let's see what's upstairs," she suggested, and once more she sounded on the verge of tears.

We went upstairs and looked in so many bedrooms I lost count. There wasn't much to choose between them; they were all large and well furnished, with comfortable beds.

"No twin size here," I observed. "Which room do you like?"

"Any of them," Jill said agreeably. For some reason that reminded me again of Marcia. She would never have responded that way. She'd have said, "I hate that one, no view." Or, "Look, we could crawl out the window of this one and drop off the roof of the lower floor onto the ground." She'd said that once when we were at my grandma's and we'd been told we couldn't go out that evening. We didn't go,

23

because I was chicken about breaking the rules and Grandma was a good friend. Grandma would like Jill, I decided.

"How about these two, the first ones at the top of the stairs?" I proposed. And then I hesitated, because what kind of way was it to spend time with a friend—I *wanted* Jill for a friend—if we were in separate rooms? "Or shall we share a bed?"

Her smile, when it came, was tentative. "I'd like that, if you wouldn't mind."

"Okay. This one, then? And Sam can have the one across the hall. I don't think we're going to get Mick to sleep in a room by himself," I said as we walked toward the head of the stairs. "Not after last night. First he thought he heard a bear, then the fire, and after that a footprint he didn't think belonged to the firemen. He's going to want to stay close to Sam."

Jill stopped, her face suddenly alert. "You think someone set that fire?"

"I don't know. I didn't want to talk to Sam about it in front of Mickey, but after a phone call where nobody spoke, to a number nobody knew because it was just put in, well, it's a funny string of coincidences. I've been watching for any signs of vandalism since we've been in the house, but I didn't see anything, did you?"

Jill shook her head. "No. Not even a broken window."

"If the kids had broken windows, I suppose they'd have replaced them right away."

"They didn't, though. I noticed the glass. It's all old."

Startled, I paused with one hand on the stair railing, not taking the first step down. "How can you tell that?"

"This is an old house, and the glass looks to be original. It was all put in a long time ago, anyway. One thing you learn, living in old dumps, is about inferior glass. The old stuff isn't as clear, it has wavy imperfections, so it distorts what you see through it. Modern glass is so clear you can't

24

tell it's there unless it's dirty. Look at that window over there, on the landing. See how wavy it looks?''

It was true. ''You looked at all the ground-floor windows? You're sure there's no new glass?''

It made me thoughtful as we went on down the stairs. Why had the Allendales suddenly hired Sam as a caretaker, after the house had been empty for a long time, if there hadn't been any vandalism?

I tried to answer my own question as we reached the ground floor. ''I didn't see any sign of damage anywhere, did you? Or where anything had been fixed recently?''

Jill shook her head. ''No. Not here. There'll be plenty to fix at the cottage, though. Do you really think it was arson? When Sam's car was right in front, so they'd have known there were people in the place?''

I laughed uneasily. ''No, probably not. I'm letting Mickey and my imagination spook me, is all.''

Still, I couldn't help wondering. Later on, when we were sitting on the edge of that gorgeous swimming pool watching Mickey and Jill splashing each other at the far end, I asked Sam if they had told him why they were hiring him.

''Did they tell you? I mean, did they mention anything specific that had happened? Or were you replacing a former caretaker?''

''They said vandalism, they wanted a stop to kids messing around up here. There wasn't any former caretaker. Nobody'd been in the cottage for ages before I opened it up,'' Sam said. He suddenly reached over and in a brotherly way shoved me into the water. ''Race you to the other end,'' he said, and did a low dive that carried him well beyond me before I could even get started.

I pushed the doubts to the back of my mind. I knew if I thought about it enough, I'd scare myself, just the way I used to when I was a little girl and Sam had told me ghost stories before he turned out my bedroom light. Once I wet the bed

25

because I was afraid to get up and go to the bathroom. Sam got bawled out when I related the ghost story to Mom. After that he wouldn't tell me any more scary stories until I promised I'd never let Mom find out.

I was fourteen years old now, for pete's sake. I wasn't going to turn chicken over nothing. Sam was nineteen, and even Dad thought he was fairly sensible. If Sam wasn't worried, why should I be?

4

We spent most of the morning in the pool. I was surprised at how different Jill was when we started horsing around in the water. She laughed and splashed Mickey and didn't seem to mind when he swam underwater and grabbed her feet and tried to pull her down.

I rested on the edge beside Sam, watching the other two. "She's really pretty, isn't she?" I observed, watching Jill in her bright blue one-piece suit.

"Yeah," Sam agreed, and gave me a lazy grin. "But don't go matching us up, Lisa. She's only a baby."

"She's fourteen," I said indignantly.

"Too young for me. Oh, I know, she keeps watching me, and turning pink every time I say anything to her. She's cute and she's nice, but she's too young. Now Beau likes even *little* girls. He saw that snapshot I have of you, and he said you were gorgeous."

"Me?" My voice squeaked, and I scrutinized him carefully to see if he was putting me on. "Are you kidding?"

"No. He said that. Of course, Beau thinks all females are gorgeous."

"Thanks a lot. Well, anyway, be nice to Jill, okay? I think her life's been kind of rough since her mom died, and she hasn't made any friends in Granite yet. Be kind."

Now it was Sam's turn to be indignant. "I'm always kind!

You're just nursing your own wounds and you see injuries to other people where there aren't any.''

"What's that supposed to mean? It's just that I know how it feels to be rejected, and I think Jill would appreciate a little kindness, is all.''

For once Sam actually appeared serious. "You're well out of that, you know. You and Marcia.''

My jaw sagged. "What are you talking about?''

"You and Marcia,'' he repeated. "For years you were practically her shadow. She's pretty, she's popular, she's a leader. You've been a follower, but you don't need to be. You're good enough to go your own way, without her.''

"Sure,'' I said glumly. "Since we broke up I don't have any friends. They're all still flocking around *her*.''

"Everybody? Come on. You had your own little clique, and everybody else wished they were part of it, but most of the kids enjoy their own groups. I used to think Marcia was a good friend to you, but this last year or so I changed my mind. She made all the decisions. You stopped making your own, you even called her up in the morning to see what to wear, for crying out loud.''

"That didn't mean anything,'' I said, stung. "Lots of girls consult with each other about clothes.''

"Clothes, and everything else. She'd say, 'Which movie shall we watch?' and you'd suggest something, and she'd say, 'No, let's watch something else,' and you always did. You never argued with her about it. You just went along with what *she* wanted to do. About everything.''

An angry denial sprang to my lips, then died before it was spoken. Had it really been that way? I guessed maybe it had, right up to the point where she let the school officials think I'd stolen that test list they found in our locker.

Was that why she'd thought she could get away with it? Because I'd fallen into the habit of doing whatever she wanted me to do?

I didn't exactly like how that made me feel.

Seemingly unaware of the turmoil he'd begun in my head, Sam was still talking. "Couldn't you see how she kept putting you down? It was like she was in competition with you to be the prettiest and most popular girl in Granite."

My voice sounded hollow. "You've got that backward. Marcia's the one who *is* the prettiest and most popular."

Sam gave an exasperated snort. "Sometimes, for a girl who's at least marginally bright, you can sure be stupid, Lisa. Marcia's loud enough and pushy enough to take the lead, and there are some people who'll always follow a girl like that. But *you* don't need to. You and Jill are both just as attractive as she is, and you're both *nicer*. Do you think Marcia would ever have invited Jill to come here with us?"

"No," I said, without thinking.

"You got that right. Marcia never thought about anybody else first in her life. You think about other people's feelings. That's more important than how you look."

Sam had never talked to me this way before. I didn't quite know how to take it.

"How come you never mentioned any of this before?"

Sam shrugged, turning his head briefly when Mickey shrieked at the other end of the pool. Jill was laughing at him, and I guessed she'd pushed him in.

"You were friends. Kind of a one-sided deal, but it wasn't any of my business. But don't go around acting as if somebody died. It's a drag for the rest of us. Besides, even if you are a pain in the neck sometimes, I kind of like you. For a sister, you're not bad. And Beau, who is a genuine connoisseur, thinks you're stunning."

I stared at him in flat disbelief, and he finally laughed.

"Have you looked in a mirror lately? Listen, I don't get my kicks seeing someone else put down, the way Marcia does. She played herself up at your expense sometimes, you know. Who needs friends like that?"

I did, I thought mournfully. When Marcia was my best friend, I'd been in the middle of everything. All the excitement, all the fun. Now I was out on the fringes, missing everything.

Sam's expression was suddenly shrewd. "Do you want her back?" he asked.

I drew in a long breath, considering. "No, I guess not."

"Good."

He had had enough of the subject, I guess. Without warning he dove into the water and swam across the pool, then hauled himself out on the far side and stood there for a moment, dripping.

"I guess it's time I went into town and called Mr. Allendale. Confessed that I wasn't the greatest watchdog last night, that his cottage is damaged, and that we've moved into the big house. I tried the phone at the cottage and it doesn't work. The one here was disconnected when the family moved out after the old man died and Mrs. Allendale went into the rest home. I went all over after breakfast, and I can't see where anything's out of order at the main house."

"You think he'll fire you?" Mickey asked, climbing out, too.

"I hope not. I was counting on the money from this job, and the time I'd have to study. But I don't know what I can do about it if he doesn't want me to stay. I'm going into town. Enjoy yourselves, in case this is your only crack at the pool."

Jill stood in the water just below my feet after Sam had gone. "It wasn't his fault there was a fire."

"No," I agreed. "But that might not stop Mr. Allendale from firing him."

"It wouldn't be fair."

"Nothing much about life is fair, as far as I can see," I said, and then, knowing I sounded self-pitying, I tried to perk up. "Come on, let's go rustle up something delicious for lunch."

30

"Macaroni and cheese," Mickey suggested, and Jill and I both laughed.

Fifteen minutes later, when I turned away from the stove where I'd just put the package-mix casserole in the oven, I saw someone moving beyond the window over the sink.

My heart leaped into my throat. Sam was gone, and that fire last night might have been arson. . . .

Then, as I leaned over for a closer look through the slightly wavy glass, I guessed who he must be.

Beau. Sam's roommate.

He was as attractive as Sam had led me to expect, though not quite in the same way. I'd pictured Beau as what Dad called an "eight-by-ten glossy": movie-star perfect.

I had a good look at him now as he stood staring toward the pool. He was an inch or so taller than Sam's six feet, and his thick dark hair had a hint of wave to it. He wore jeans and a polo shirt with casual elegance, a jacket held over his shoulder with one raised finger.

This was the guy who thought I was attractive? Unless Sam had been putting me on, of course. Just talking to make me feel better.

Beau was good-looking, all right, though not in a flashy way. He looked . . . friendly, approachable. Anyway, as approachable as any boy my own age would be.

My heart rate speeded up. I lifted a hand to knock on the glass to catch his attention, but he was already leaving, striding in an athletic way toward the front of the house.

Since he hadn't seen Sam's car, he'd probably thought there was nobody here. I turned to hurry through the big formal dining room with the table that could seat twenty people and into the broad corridor that led to the front door. I felt a little self-conscious after what my brother had said, but kind of anticipated meeting Beau, too. Maybe part of what Sam had said was true.

Jill was coming downstairs as I reached the entryway on the run. "Is something happening?" she asked.

"It's Beau—wouldn't you know he'd come when Sam isn't here?"

It didn't bother me, though. I felt as if I already sort of knew my brother's roommate, and maybe he was looking forward to meeting me, too.

I tripped over a suitcase Mickey hadn't put away, regained my balance, and pulled open the multipaneled front door.

The guy was just getting into a silvery-gray sports car, his back to me.

"Beau! Wait!" I cried, but he didn't hear me. A moment later, before I'd even reached the bottom of the steps, waving wildly in hope he'd at least see me in the rearview mirror, he was driving away.

Jill came out onto the veranda behind me. "Isn't he going to stay?"

"He didn't see me! He probably stopped at the cottage and saw all the mess, and then when there was no car in sight up here, he figured we'd left!" I felt limp with disappointment.

"He'll be back," Jill predicted. "Maybe he'll meet Sam on the road or in town."

"I hope so. Did you get a look at him?"

Jill grinned. "No. Was he as handsome as Sam says?"

"More so. Attractive, rather than . . . pretty. Didn't you get the impression from Sam that he was almost too good to be true?"

Jill was still grinning, and I saw that Sam was right. She was cute, and she was nice. "Obviously you didn't think so. Don't worry, Lisa, he knows this is where Sam is spending the summer. He'll be back."

I supposed she was right, but it seemed such a waste for Beau to leave before I'd had a chance to meet him when Sam wasn't there. If Sam reverted to form, he'd probably say something to embarrass me.

We went back into the house. Mickey met us in the front hall wearing only shorts. "I'm going back in the woods to see if I can find the pond. Sam says there must be one, where all the frogs are croaking. If you make a cake, be sure to save me my share."

I looked after him, laughing. "If I make a cake! Why should you think I'd do that, when we brought all those packages of cookies with us? I told you, Jill, we were along strictly as cooks and bottle washers!"

"I don't mind. Well, since we've moved into this house, we don't have to wash up, anyway. It'll be nice having a dishwasher. Do you think we could uncover the furniture in one room where we can sit down?"

"I don't see why not. If Mr. Allendale fires Sam, we'll just have to cover things up again."

"And go home," Jill said, sounding subdued.

"Well, we'll have Mrs. Gottman to deal with if that happens," I said, "but the way she looks I'll bet she can cook. And there are twin beds in my room, so you can stay with us until your dad comes back from his business trip. We can find something to do even back home."

We choked on the dust when we pulled the covers off the furniture in the study, but by the time we finished in there I was glad we'd done it. It was a beautiful room.

"Ordinary people lived here," Jill said, pausing before a cluster of old photos on the wall opposite the fireplace. "See, here's a whole family. And there's one of the gardener, I guess, and a little boy. Look at this lady, isn't she pretty?"

"A nice-looking family," I agreed. "I suppose they were ordinary, except for being rich."

Jill gave a final swipe at the glass door on a bookcase. "Can't you be rich and be a nice regular family at the same time?"

33

Well, there's no way *our* family could be called rich," I said, "so I'm no expert on that. I guess Beau's folks are rich. And Sam says he's a regular sort of person, fun to be with, considerate, that kind of thing. I wish I'd managed to stop him from leaving. This looks great, we can come in here this evening and entertain in style. What'll we do now?"

"Go swimming again? It's easy to *pretend* we're rich, with a house like this and that big pool."

So we went upstairs to change back into bathing suits. Sam had told us we should rinse them out and dry them after each wearing, because of the chlorine. There hadn't been that much else to do (and there was a washer and dryer downstairs), so we'd actually done that and put our suits away.

I probably wouldn't have bothered with dresser drawers instead of using things out of my suitcase, but Jill sort of put me to shame. She wasn't obsessively neat, yet when she lined her stuff up in the drawers, I figured I might as well do that, too.

I pulled open the top drawer and drew in a sharp breath.

"Something wrong?" Jill was staring at me, her hand on the drawer knob on her side of the dresser.

"Yeah," I said slowly. "I didn't leave things in a mess like this." For a moment I wondered if *she* had poked around in my stuff, and then I knew by her face that she hadn't.

Jill moistened her lips, then pulled open her own drawer and looked at a similar jumble of underwear, socks, and bathing suits.

"Somebody's been looking through our things," she said, incredulous. Her voice had an odd note. "Mickey wouldn't have been in here, would he? I mean, no, of course he wouldn't, but—" She broke off, embarrassed.

"I never knew Mickey to poke around in other people's stuff," I said, figuring if he had I was going to kill him.

Jill lifted her bathing suit out of the tangled mess. "Are we still going to go swimming?" she asked uncertainly.

34

I sighed. "I guess so. Let's change and then I'll get some towels."

I went to the door of the bathroom off the hall and felt my feet becoming rooted to the floor.

Right beside me, Jill made a strangled sound.

It was a luxurious bath, done in pale green tile, with lots of mirrors. Sam had set out a shaving kit, which had been emptied into the bathtub; shaving cream had been sprayed out across the surrounding tile. Toothbrushes and toothpaste had been dumped together in the sink, and there was a red smear on the edge of the vanity that sent prickles racing over my bare skin.

Jill found her voice before I found mine. "Is it . . . blood?"

For a moment I couldn't move, could hardly even breathe. I reached for the tissue box that had been knocked to the floor. Dampening one of the tissues, I rubbed tentatively at one end of the red stain and swallowed hard before answering.

"It sure looks like it. As if somebody cut himself on that broken glass—see, it's in the wastebasket. It couldn't have been Mickey. He'd have used up all the Band-Aids on a cut. Besides, he always tells everybody about the least little injury."

Jill's tongue moved slowly over her lips. "It couldn't have been Sam. We've been in here since he left for town."

"So who was it?" I wondered aloud. The prickling now extended all the way down my spine. "I guess we better not touch anything until Sam sees this. He's supposed to be here to prevent this kind of thing. How did anybody get in?"

We stared at each other, and I could see goose bumps on her arms, too. Jill flicked a glance down the long corridor, with all those doors opening from it.

"Let's go outside until Sam gets back," she said in a rush, and I didn't argue.

35

Forgetting about swimming or towels, we practically ran down the stairs.

At the back door that led from the kitchen onto a rear terrace, I stopped so abruptly that Jill ran into me.

"What's the matter now?"

I was short of breath, and not from running. "The back door. It isn't locked. Nobody's been in or out this way, have they? Mickey left by the front door, and Sam did, too."

Jill shivered. "Come on, let's get out of here!"

5

It was warm and peaceful in the backyard, but we no longer felt like swimming. We sat on the edge of the pool, facing the house, and dangled our feet in the water. The way Jill's gaze kept drifting from one end of the house to the other made it clear she was as uneasy as I was.

"I hope Sam gets back soon," I muttered. "And Beau too. I don't think I like being here by ourselves."

When Sam arrived a short time later, however, he was alone.

He strode across the lawn toward us, lifting a hand in greeting. "Well, I'm not fired. Everett Allendale was upset about the fire, but he said he'd turn the matter over to his insurance company, and that it was okay to move into the big house. He said to make sure nobody got in there."

I had a cramp in the pit of my stomach. "They already have," I told him soberly as Sam dropped down on his haunches beside us.

Sam went very still. "What do you mean? What happened?"

I explained, watching his face.

"You ask Mick if he had anything to do with any of this?"

"No, but I'm sure he didn't. He's out looking for the frog pond. We yelled at him from the edge of the woods, and he yelled back and said he'd found a snake. Jill doesn't like snakes, so we left him out there. I thought he'd be safe; anybody'd have to go through here to get back there.''

He accepted my hint that maybe we could be in danger here, so I went on. "You didn't meet Beau anywhere?''

"No, did he show up? I didn't expect him yet; he was going down to Coos Bay to fish for a couple of days first.''

"I tried to run out and tell him we were here, but he got away before I could get from the back of the house to the front door.''

"Well, he'll come back. Come on, maybe you better show me what this mysterious invader's done. And then I'll check all the doors and windows, secure the place. Maybe someone was careless and left that back door unlocked, so the vandals had a way to get in easily. If the lock doesn't work, I'll replace it and charge it to Mr. Allendale.''

There was nothing wrong with the lock. Two windows were found unlatched; Sam locked them and went on to inspect the others. "Nobody'll get in again,'' he assured us, and then we led him upstairs to show him the mess in the bathroom as well as our disturbed belongings.

I felt a little better by the time we came back downstairs; just having Sam there helped a lot. "It was probably kids, messing around,'' he said. "I'll make sure they don't get in again.''

Mickey came in smelling sort of swampy; he'd captured a huge frog, which he displayed in a wicker basket he'd picked up behind the stable.

"I decided to leave the snake,'' he said, gloating over the frog.

"Just don't get him near the pool,'' Sam warned. "Remember, we'll have to clean it out before we leave. Their old pool man came out and got it ready for us, but he only comes once a month when the family isn't here. Let's have a quick swim before we eat, okay?''

By dinnertime that evening Beau still hadn't reappeared.

Jill, who was more domestic than I was, offered to do the cooking if I'd do the cleanup later. She loved baking things and fixing fancy stuff.

"Too bad Beau's missing this," I observed when she served Boston cream pie for dessert. "What do you think happened to him?"

Sam cut a second sliver of the cake. "Don't worry about Beau. He's well able to take care of himself. He probably met somebody interesting—most likely a pretty girl—but he'll show up eventually. He knows I didn't expect him for a few days yet."

We spent the evening playing Scrabble with a game we found in the billiards room (Sam won three games in a row, just as I'd predicted) and then Sam taught Jill to shoot pool.

I watched, enjoying Jill's obvious pleasure and Sam's funny comments. Mickey fell asleep in a big chair, halfway through an old movie on TV, and Sam hauled him upstairs when the rest of us decided to go to bed.

I hadn't been nervous at all until then, but now the house seemed huge, and even when we turned the lights on everywhere, there were deep shadows that made my skin crawl. We'd cleaned up the mess in the bathroom, but I remembered it clearly, and what it meant: Someone had invaded our privacy, and even if it was only kids, that was unsettling.

"What if Beau comes again? Should we leave a light on, just in case?" I asked.

Sam paused on the staircase. "Leave the outside light on if you want to, though I doubt he'll come this late at night. Don't worry, he knows there are two pretty girls here; he'll show up tomorrow." He grinned and went on upstairs.

Disgruntled, I snorted, "He sounds too girl crazy—and too undiscriminating—to matter anyway."

Jill and I followed Sam up, and we decided to leave the hall light on. Not because we were scared of the dark, of course. Just to make sure anyone who needed the bathroom could find it easily in this unfamiliar house.

Jill was actually quite relaxed and talkative as we got ready for bed. She kept talking about Sam. As we slid into our sleeping bags, side by side, she laughed self-consciously.

"I sound like an idiot, don't I? I know Sam's too old for me, and he thinks I'm a baby. If there'd been girls his own age around, he'd never have looked at me twice. But he's fun, and he was nice to me. It's been such a long time since I've really had fun."

That made me feel guilty. I'd always had fun—well, almost always—until the split with Marcia. "We'll think of some more fun things to do," I promised, and heard her sleepy, "Sure. I'm glad you invited me, Lisa. Good night."

I was surprised to wake up the next morning and realize nothing had happened that was frightening. The sun was streaming in the windows, I heard Sam whistling in the bathroom, and I was starved.

Jill opened her eyes when I rolled toward her. "Shall I make an omelet for breakfast? I haven't made one in a long time, but my mom taught me how."

I bounded out of bed with enthusiasm. "Great! Omelet and toast with strawberry jam! Let's go!"

She was pretty good in the kitchen. I never heard anybody quite so enthusiastic; the oven was perfect, the toaster was a super four-slice one, there was an omelet pan and a little device for slicing mushrooms. As for me, somebody else was doing the cooking, so I didn't mind scraping off the plates and putting them in the dishwasher.

Mickey couldn't wait to eat and be gone. "The pond is really neat," he burbled. "There're all kinds of things living around it. Besides the frogs and snakes and dragonflies, I saw some tracks I think might be a fox. I sure hope I get to see the fox."

"It's pretty tricky to creep up on a wild animal," Sam

40

warned him. "Your best bet is to sit in absolute silence near where you saw the tracks by the water. Even then it will probably smell you."

"I'm going to rub sage all over me," Mickey stated. "There's a patch of it in the garden out back. That's what Grandpa does when he's going in the woods. He says he just smells like a garden, and the deer don't pay any attention."

Sam had questioned him last night and we knew he hadn't had anything to do with the mess upstairs or the unlocked back door. Sam kept it casual, and Mickey didn't seem perturbed, but as he wiped the last of the orange juice off his upper lip and headed out the back door, I spoke quietly.

"You think he'll be okay out there by himself? If there's someone prowling around?"

"Nobody's going to bother a little kid out in the woods," Sam said. "It's so far from a road, and with the wall around this place the only way they could get there is right through the yard. There isn't even another gate except a little one in the far corner, and it's been locked so long it's rusted shut. I tried it. Mick'll be okay. Besides, the pond's close enough so we could hear him yell if he needed help."

I looked at him without arguing, hoping he was right. I wasn't sure Mom would think so, not after the signs we'd found that someone had been in the house. Had that someone come right past us, through the yard, and we simply hadn't seen him?

"What did Mr. Allendale say when he hired you, Sam? Did he expect you'd have to deal with people who could be dangerous?"

"All he said was kids had gotten in and broken some things. Windows, I think. Nothing serious."

"Jill says there haven't been any broken windows. All the glass is old, the kind with flaws in it. Like that one—when you stand over here you can see that it distorts what you're

41

looking at. There's no new glass anywhere in the house; we checked yesterday while you were in town."

Sam gave Jill a thoughtful look. "You're pretty perceptive to notice a thing like that. You're right, new glass would be clearer. Well, I don't know. I just assumed he meant the kids had broken a window to get in. Maybe he didn't actually say so. I can't remember."

"We didn't see any signs that anything had been damaged, and we were all over the place while you were gone. Except for the stuff dumped around in the bathroom. Why would anyone have done that?"

Sam shrugged, drained the juice from his glass, and stood up. "Who knows why kids do anything? Rebellion against authority, boredom, so that stupid things seem entertaining. Anyway, the windows are all locked on the ground floor. We'll be sure the doors are locked, too. I doubt if we have anything to worry about."

"What about the fire?" I persisted, unable to accept his evaluation of our situation. "If I hadn't woken up when I did, we might have been killed. There was a footprint behind the cottage that didn't match those boots the firemen were wearing, and someone could have reached inside the front windows and set the drapes afire. We all thought Mickey was imagining a bear in the bushes, but what if there was a *person* out there?"

"Why would anyone want to burn us up? Fires start accidentally all the time, Lisa."

"Enough of it burned to get pretty scary," I remembered aloud.

"Maybe someone just wanted us to leave," Jill suggested unexpectedly.

Sam gave her a quizzical look. "You figured out why anyone would take such a drastic means to do it?"

Jill flushed. "No. But it worked. We got out of the gatekeeper's place. And then when we moved in here, whoever

42

it was messed up the bathroom and looked through our things. Maybe to scare us away from here, too.''

"You scared enough to want to go home?'' Sam asked.

Jill shook her head. "Not if the rest of you are staying. Not if the doors are locked now so whoever it was can't get in again.''

I was almost sorry she hadn't said she wanted to go home. He hadn't asked *me*.

"Well, I'm going to look around pretty carefully,'' Sam said. "Make sure it's safe. Mr. Allendale hired a caretaker, not an armed guard. If there's some weirdo running loose who's dangerous, I'm not getting paid enough to take care of that. If he wants a real security guard, he'd better hire someone with a gun and the experience to use it. Listen, Lisa, Beau's bound to show up today. If you're serious about impressing him, he *loves* chocolate cake.''

"And you don't, I suppose,'' I teased, willing to be diverted, though I wasn't all that sure that a guy who could so easily be distracted by one girl after another was worth worrying about. Not that Beau would really consider me as a girlfriend, anyway.

I hoped Sam was right in his appraisal of the situation. If he wasn't worried, did I need to be?

He was grinning. "Oh, if you twist my arm I'd probably eat a piece. I'll let Jill try it first, just to make sure it won't poison me.'' Sam dodged the elbow I aimed at his ribs and laughingly let himself out the back door.

By noon, with the chocolate cake from a mix sitting on the counter awaiting Beau's arrival, there was no sign of our expected guest.

There was no sign of Sam, either.

Mickey came in from the pond, reeking of stagnant water and slimy things. "Have you seen Sam?'' I asked as he scrubbed his hands at the kitchen sink.

43

"Nope. Just a redheaded woodpecker and a bunch of blue jays, besides the frogs. We don't have to wait for Sam to eat, do we?"

"No, I guess not. Come on, sit down. Sam will show up when he's ready."

But Sam didn't come.

Jill offered to cook supper—scalloped potatoes with ham from a can—and went about it between evident enjoyment at the task and uncertain glances at me. "Maybe he went to town for something," she offered once.

"He couldn't have. The station wagon's still here."

At first I was exasperated with my brother. How could he be so inconsiderate as not to let us know what was going on? And not showing up when it was time to eat was definitely not like Sam.

By the time the potatoes came out of the oven, we should have been hungry, but nobody was.

"I don't know what we ought to do," I said, looking at the beautiful meal. "This isn't like Sam."

The light had begun to fade; the big trees made heavy shadows around the house; exasperation became alarm.

"Maybe we should search for him," Mickey proposed. "Before it gets all the way dark. Are you sure he's still out-doors?"

So we did that, though we didn't go far from the house, only to the edge of the woods and down by the caretaker's cottage, where the acrid smell of burned wood and fabric made my nose sting. There was nothing to suggest that Sam had been there.

We didn't think he could have come inside without anyone seeing him, but we walked all over the big house, the three of us together, without mentioning that we were too scared to split up. Except for our own echoing footsteps, we heard nothing and saw only empty rooms.

44

We were alone, Jill and Mickey and I, and it was getting dark now.

I had to face it. Sam had disappeared.

6

Jill's nice dinner was cold, and nobody wanted to eat anyway. We were too scared.

"What are we going to do?" Mickey asked, his freckles standing out starkly on a pale face.

I swallowed hard. I'd never been on my own in a situation like this before, and the responsibility was too big for me.

I looked at Jill, who was soberly waiting for me to take charge. "Can you drive a car?"

"I've watched my dad. I never tried to do it," she said.

Mick tugged at my arm. "I've watched, too, Lisa! I know how!"

"So have I watched, and never done it, and I'm tall enough to see over the steering wheel. It's automatic," I said hopefully, "so maybe we could get to town and contact the sheriff's office."

"If Sam's not really missing and you call the cops," Mickey said, "he'll be real mad at us."

"If he's not really missing, I'll be real mad at *him*," I said, "for scaring us this way. I wish there was a working phone in this place. We can't call unless we go to town."

"We going to call Mom and Dad?"

"How? They're in Brussels now, and we know the name of the hotel, but not the phone number. Besides, they expected to be at the convention the first three days, and I don't know if it's day or night over there right now. What could they do, anyway? We'd just make them scared, too, and Mom would probably feel she had to fly home immediately and ruin their whole trip. No, we'll just talk to the sheriff. Let's see if Sam left the keys in the car.''

We trooped out together to see. He hadn't, so it didn't matter whether any of us could drive or not.

''Maybe there are neighbors,'' Jill said tentatively, and then after a look at my face she sort of deflated. ''No, I guess not. We didn't see any close by on the way in, did we?''

''It must be five or six miles back to the main highway. There's a house there, I think, where we turned off. Shall we walk back there? We've walked that far before, Mick, when we hiked on Mount Pilchuck.''

Mickey glanced at the blackness beyond the windows. ''In the dark?'' he asked.

At the same time Jill said, ''I remember the house at the corner. A big brown one, wasn't it? There was a For Sale sign on it, and I think it was empty. I mean, there weren't any curtains or lights, and it was dusk.''

''So we could walk all that way and still not find a phone or anybody with a car.'' I said, sounding hollow. I sort of felt that way, too.

It was clear that Jill and Mickey were waiting for me to decide what to do, and I didn't know. If only Beau would show up!

He didn't.

''Sam didn't take the car, so he *must* be on the place,'' I said in desperation.

''Where?''

The word hung in the air without an answer.

''I feel like we should keep looking for him,'' I said, hearing my voice waver. ''But if we didn't find him before it got dark, what chance would we have now?''

Nobody answered that, either.

In the end we decided—or I suggested and the other two

agreed—that we'd have to wait until morning. Then, if Sam hadn't turned up, or Beau, we'd start walking to town, a telephone, and the police.

I could have kicked myself for not setting out to search immediately when Sam didn't show up for lunch. Maybe then we might have seen footprints, or broken branches in the woods, something to indicate which way he'd gone.

I didn't think there was much chance I'd sleep, but I did, though badly. Mickey had moved his sleeping bag into our room and the light was on again in the hallway.

Once I woke with a pounding heart, convinced I'd heard footsteps. "Sam?" I called out tentatively, but there was no response.

After a moment to gather my courage, I slipped out of bed and tiptoed across the hall, sweeping across the room with the beam of the flashlight. Sam's bed was empty, exactly as I had last seen it.

My eyes stung as I returned to bed. The dread was growing in me until it threatened to choke off my breath, and I curled up inside my sleeping bag and prayed that it was nearly daylight.

If only Beau would come! He was older, he'd know what to do better than I did, and he had a car.

What could have happened to Sam?

All I knew was that it had to be bad, or he'd be here where he belonged, taking charge.

I woke hearing little birds in the tree outside the window. Mickey and Jill were still sound asleep, but I couldn't stay here a minute longer. I felt so guilty about Sam; how could I have slept at all, with Sam missing, not knowing what had happened to him?

I dressed hurriedly and pulled a sweater over my short-sleeved shirt, then moved across the hall to check on Sam's room. I'd known Sam wouldn't be there, but disappointment was a painful ache in my chest. What could possibly have happened to my brother? And what was I going to do about it?

The police, I thought. They were equipped to find missing people.

As I turned away from Sam's empty bed, Mickey's tousled head emerged from his sleeping bag. "Did Sam come back yet?"

My throat hurt. "No."

"If we can't call Mom and Dad, shall we call Grandpa and Grandma?"

"Not yet," I decided as Jill raised up on an elbow to face me. "They couldn't do anything but worry. We'll make a more thorough search this morning. Then if we don't find him, we'll walk to town and notify the police."

For long seconds Mickey stared into my face. "You don't think somebody killed him, do you?"

I'd been trying not to think about such a possibility, and I spoke hastily. "No, of course not. He might have gotten hurt, though, and couldn't get home." Guilt that I hadn't taken his disappearance more seriously, much sooner, pushed me to the verge of tears. "Maybe he fell or something, and broke a leg or . . ."

My voice trailed off. If it had been Mickey, or me, Sam would never have left us lying injured in the woods overnight. He'd have called out the Search and Rescue Unit before dark.

"Get dressed," I said, "and we'll look again before we head for town."

Mickey and Jill were both downstairs by the time I'd heated the water for cocoa. We didn't take time to drink all of that, even. We were silent as we headed out of the house until we reached the edge of the pool. "We forgot to cover it last night," I said, for there was a leaf floating on the surface of

49

the blue-green water. "Well, I guess we've got more important things to do right now."

"Where do we start?" Jill asked.

I wasn't used to being the leader, I thought wildly. If Marcia were there, she'd be deciding the course of action. If Sam were there, it went without saying that he would take the lead.

But Sam was missing, Mom and Dad were in Europe, and Grandpa and Grandma were in Bellingham, over an hour's drive away.

There was only me.

And then I heard the car. Driving in here, at the front of the house.

I ran around the corner of the house, Mickey and Jill trailing, to see the silvery-gray sports car and the tall figure getting out of it.

I was so relieved I didn't even introduce myself or wait for him to speak.

"Beau! I'm so glad you came back! I saw you yesterday when you were here, but you drove off before I could get to the door—"

Puffing, I came to a stop in front of him. He was even more attractive than I'd thought yesterday, but I didn't have time to think about that now.

"Sam's disappeared," I blurted, unable to control the tremor in my voice.

"Disappeared?" He echoed the word rather blankly. "In the—" He turned to glance toward the cottage that was hidden in the trees.

"No, no, we got out of that all right and moved into the main house. Sam went out after breakfast yesterday to look around, to see if he could find any sign that anyone was breaking into the house or doing anything they shouldn't be, and he just . . . never came back."

The newcomer was staring at me. "Never came back,"

50

he echoed. "Sorry, I sound like a parrot, don't I? You mean he's been gone since yesterday morning?"

I was so grateful for his presence that I couldn't seem to stop babbling. "Yes. At first I thought he was busy finding clues or something, and then for a while I even wondered if he were playing a joke on us. He knew we were scared after the fire—I'll tell you about that later, maybe it was arson—and someone was in the house yesterday, too, pawed through our belongings and made a mess in the bathroom—"

I had to pause for breath, and I was humiliated to know that I not only must have sounded like an idiot but I was nearly crying. I didn't want him to think I was hysterical. Guys have trouble dealing with hysterical females. I knew that much from listening to Sam and his friends.

I pulled myself together. "Beau—I'm sorry, that sounds so forward, when we haven't even been introduced, but Sam always called you Beau; I don't even know your real name, just your nickname. Do they always call you that?"

He blinked, then replied cordially enough, "Well, I really prefer being called by my name. It's Dan. Dan Campton. Look, I can see you're upset, and I don't blame you. Where did you last see . . . uh, Sam? Let's see what we can do about that."

So much for trying to be a leader, I thought, almost falling-down limp at the idea of handing over the whole problem to someone better prepared than I was to deal with an emergency. I'd learn the leadership skills later, I vowed inwardly. Right now I wanted help finding Sam.

Explanations poured out of me as we all headed toward the rear terrace. "This is the door Sam left by," I said, pausing there. "We don't know for sure which direction he went. We looked for footprints or any other signs, but we didn't find anything."

Dan—I liked that better than a silly nickname like Beau, I decided—immediately took charge, as I'd known he would.

51

No doubt later I'd wish I'd been more forceful, but this being a leader took time to learn, didn't it?

"Well, it doesn't look as if it's rained recently, so probably there won't be much in the way of footprints, unless they're back in the woods or at least in the edge of the trees. First let's make a pass around the cleared area, check to see if there's grass flattened or any sign he passed that way. Did you check out the stable?"

"No. We didn't get around to searching last night until it was actually dark, and we only have one small flashlight." Once more guilt washed over me. Poor Sam, wherever he was, waiting for us—*trusting us*—to find him, and we hadn't done it. "We yelled from here, though, and he didn't answer."

It sounded lame, inadequate. I couldn't be making a very good impression on Beau—no, Dan. I had a notion that when we found Sam, if he was all right, he was going to tell me everything I should have done that I either hadn't thought of or had been too timid to do, and after that he'd strangle me.

"Mickey and I can check the edge of the woods for prints," Jill volunteered. "If you two want to do the stable."

We split up into pairs. I had to trot to keep up with Dan's longer steps as he started purposefully toward the barn.

It was obvious that the building hadn't been used in years. Unlike the main house and the gatekeeper's cottage, the stable had fallen into a state of disrepair. The wide door resisted Dan's initial effort to open it until he threw his full weight against the end of it. Then it slid aside with a protesting shriek of metal on rusted metal.

The sunlight penetrated only a yard or so into the interior. Dan moved without hesitation into the deep shadows; I followed him more slowly, letting my eyes adjust to the dimness. My heart was beating very rapidly, though I didn't see how my brother could be in there. If Sam had entered through that door, he wouldn't have closed it until he left.

52

There seemed little to fear here once I could see clearly. It wasn't as dark as it had at first seemed; light came through another open doorway at the far end of the building, through various dusty windows, and one shaft struck directly to the floor ahead of us through a hole in the roof.

I sounded nervous. "Boy, they must have had a lot of horses at one time. Look at the box stalls."

"Twenty-five or thirty, anyway," Dan confirmed. "Let's open them up, make sure they're all empty."

We each took one side of the barn, opening the stall doors to peer inside. There was nothing but a little ancient hay that gave off a musty odor.

It scared me to think that Sam might be here, but it scared me more to think he wasn't. Because then where was he, and what did we do next?

Dan had paused at the foot of a wooden ladder that led upward into more semidarkness. Another stray band of sunlight caught him across the side of the face, highlighting strong features and the crisp dark hair. "This feels kind of shaky. I don't know if it's safe to climb it or not. He could have gone up there, though. What was he looking for, exactly?"

"Anything to indicate there was someone around, someone who didn't belong here."

Dan stepped back from the ladder, glancing around and then bending to pick up something off the floor. It was a crumpled candy-bar wrapper. "Would Sam have had this? It doesn't look as if it's been here for long. Certainly not for as long as the house had been closed up."

I shook my head. "I don't think so. I brought a few candy bars, but my mom was bearing down on healthy foods, so I mostly picked cookies and granola bars and fruit for snacks. Besides, you know Sam. He loves plain chocolate, but he doesn't like raisins and nuts in it, like this one. It isn't the kind of candy he'd pick for himself."

"Someone else, then. Could be just kids, fooling around."

But why had Sam disappeared, I wondered, if it was only kids?

There was a tack room, vacant except for the spiders in the corners, and a grain room, and a small office. None of them showed any sign that they'd been disturbed in years.

Dan shouldered his way through the doorway that opened at the far end of the barn into a series of corrals that had once been painted white. Now the paint was flaking and the cross-bars sagged.

I emerged from the doorway into blinding sunlight when I heard Dan's low exclamation.

"What . . . oh, no!" I choked on the cry.

We had found Sam.

He lay in a crumpled heap against the wall of the barn, curled forward, one hand thrown out and lifeless.

We had circled the barn last night, from a distance, but hadn't approached close enough to see a sprawled figure in the deep grass. The guilt became agony; Sam had lain here for hours without medical help because I was too chicken to check out a big old rotting building in the dark. It didn't help that I had never imagined something like this, that he'd had been hurt so bad he couldn't answer us. I should have checked here long before this.

I couldn't ask the terrible question.

Dan knelt beside Sam's limp body. "He's not dead, but he's sure knocked out cold." He looked upward to where a doorway opened above us from the loft; just below the door a heavy chain dangled from a pulley arrangement, a chain with a big metal hook on the end of it for lifting hay into the loft. "He may have fallen from there," Dan said. "He either cracked his head on the way down or when he hit. I hope he didn't connect with that concrete foundation."

I dropped to my knees and reached for Sam's hand; it was cool, but not cold. I spoke around the lump in my throat.

"He's been here a long time. Probably since noon, at least, yesterday. It's a bad sign, isn't it, that he's still unconscious?"

I wouldn't cry, I thought. I *wouldn't*.

Dan was frowning. "There's a bad bruise on this side of his forehead. His arm's at a funny angle, too. I think maybe his shoulder's dislocated. We'd better get him to a doctor. I noticed the sign in Arlington for a hospital when I came through there. You want to stay here with him? I'll drive out to get him."

"Do you think it's safe to move him?"

Dan hesitated. "I could go to town and call an aide car, I guess. There's no sign of a neck or spinal injury, though, and those are the things that make it dangerous to move an injured person. We'd get medical attention for him a lot quicker if we took him in ourselves. Are the keys in the station wagon? It would be easier to transport him in that than in my silver streak."

"He had the keys on him, I think." Gingerly, I probed my brother's pocket and came up with the key chain. "We've got sleeping bags we can spread in the back of the car to put him on."

Tears wouldn't help Sam, I thought, and bit into my lower lip before I blurted anxiously, "Do you think he'll be all right? He's pretty badly hurt, isn't he?"

"Well, if he's been unconscious since yesterday, he's not in too great shape," Dan admitted. "But his pulse is strong. I'll be back as soon as I can." He took the keys and rounded the corner of the barn at a sprint.

I crouched beside Sam, looking at the still face. I'd mostly taken him for granted; at times I'd resented his teasing and his practical jokes and the fact that being five years older gave him so many privileges I was denied.

I squeezed his hand and spoke softly. "Don't die, Sam.

Hang on. Beau's here, and we'll take care of you. You'll be all right. You have to be all right.''

I didn't realize that tears were running down my cheeks until they dripped onto my bare arm, and then I choked on a sob. Would anybody ever forgive me for not finding him sooner? Would I ever forgive myself?

I heard the station wagon coming before it eased around the end of the barn, backing toward us. Jill was out of it, with Mickey right behind her; she was running before Dan turned off the ignition, falling to her knees beside me, her face white.

"Oh, no! Oh, Lisa, it's bad, isn't it?"

A painful lump in my throat made it impossible to reply. She squeezed my arm and for a few moments my vision blurred so that her face wasn't clear. Mickey's eyes were wide and shocked, begging me for a reassurance I couldn't give.

And then Dan was there, opening the rear of the wagon. He knelt again by Sam, hands examining arms and legs and body. "We'll do this very carefully. I improvised a stretcher out of this lawn chair, and we'll move him as little as possible. I've been on the volunteer fire department, and I've watched the Emergency Medical technicians do this quite a few times. I'll take his head and you two lift his feet.''

Dan was as competent as I'd expected him to be. We lifted Sam into the back of the station wagon, then all piled in with Dan for the trip to town.

All the way there I prayed that Sam would be all right and I wouldn't have to make a terrible phone call to Brussels that would bring my folks home in a state of either panic or grief.

I had a fleeting thought that we'd abandoned Allendale and if someone was fooling around now was his chance to get at whatever he wanted, but there was nothing any of us could do about that.

The important thing was getting Sam to a hospital.

7

When we took seats in the small waiting room, Dan said quietly, "Let's not panic about this until after the doctor's seen him, okay? Lots of people get knocked out without doing any permanent damage."

"When we know, then can I panic?" I asked with a sort of watery smile. As jokes go, it wasn't much; I knew Sam would have managed better. Dan grinned gratefully.

He had a reputation for liking girls, but not blubbery ones. Which was what I would probably turn into if the news wasn't good when the doctor came out of the Emergency Room.

"Sure. In the meantime, tell me again just what's been going on out there, in detail."

I was more coherent this time. I still cringed, thinking how I must have sounded when he first showed up at Allendale, but he didn't seem to be holding it against me.

Dan listened intently, asking a question once in a while. He didn't ask why I had been so stupid once Sam had failed to show up, and I liked him for that. The whole time we talked, we were all aware of the activity in the small hospital. Nurses' aides pushing wheelchairs or gurneys, old people and young mothers with children, and a teenage boy with his hand wrapped in a bloody bandage went past us and into various rooms. Most of them came out again and still nobody approached us.

I finished my recital of the facts, hesitated, then plunged

57

on. "I'd have felt silly saying this except for what happened to Sam. I think the fire was set, and someone was definitely in the house besides us. Maybe they even did something to Sam, maybe he didn't fall. I can't think why he'd have been up in that loft unless he . . . heard someone up there."

I gulped for air and asked the question that was, apart from Sam's condition, uppermost in my mind. "You are going to be able to stay on with us, aren't you? Until you go home to Boston? Sam said your folks won't be there for a couple of weeks yet."

Dan hesitated, and I felt my chest get all tight, and then he gave me a slight smile. "I wouldn't go off without finding out how this comes out," he said, and some of the tension eased, but only for a moment.

The door to the room where they'd taken Sam swung open, and the doctor came toward us.

He didn't look like a doctor. He hardly seemed older than Sam and was much smaller; I suspected that he wore the dark beard to make himself appear more mature.

He wasn't wearing a white coat, either, but a plaid western-style shirt with jeans. Involuntarily, I glanced downward and saw the cowboy boots, real ones that were scuffed as if from stirrups.

"Hi, I'm Dr. Lansing," he greeted us. "Which one of you's his sister?"

"I am." I sounded squeaky. "Is . . . is he going to be okay?"

Jill had moved close to me, reaching for my hand, and I clung to her, hardly able to breathe.

"Oh, yes, I think so. There's no skull fracture, though he does have a severe concussion. He has a dislocated collarbone and a fractured ulna—that's this large bone here—" he demonstrated on his own arm—"and we have an orthopedist, Dr. Henry, coming in to set that." There was curiosity on his face. "How did he come to fall?"

58

"We don't know. Nobody was there when it happened."
I was shaking now that I wouldn't have to track my parents
down and call them home with terrible news. "It looked as
if maybe he fell out of the hayloft."

Dr. Lansing consulted the form on his clipboard, frowning. "This says your parents are in Europe?"

My heart was suddenly racing again. "Yes. For a month.
We gave the lady in the front office the letter my mom signed,
for permission to treat any of us if we needed medical attention. Do we need to notify them?"

"Well, most parents react badly to this kind of surprise,"
he said. "Sounds like yours had the foresight to prepare you
for an emergency; without that letter of permission, we'd
have been quite limited in what we could do, unless we got
a court order for it, and that's usually reserved for life-and-
death cases. That doesn't apply here, luckily."

He suddenly grinned, looking even younger. "I'll tell you
what I'd do, off the record. I wouldn't try to call them, I'd
write. You know where to write to?"

I gulped. "We have the address of the hotel."

"Right. Tell them that he had a fall and needed to be in
the hospital for a few days—it probably won't be much more
than that—but that he's coming along okay. They can hear
the grisly details later, after the crisis is over."

"Is . . . is the crisis over?" I asked.

"Well, after we get him patched up we're going to admit
him for observation. That's pretty much standard procedure
with a head injury, and we'd certainly want to do it in this
instance, where your parents aren't going to be with him
when he leaves. There's always a slight chance there may be
something we haven't caught, and if he's here where we can
watch him, we can head off any problems. He's beginning
to come around, though he's disoriented and isn't making
much sense. So far he's just muttering gibberish, but my
guess is that'll pass fairly quickly. Would you like to see him

59

before Dr. Mancowski gets here? It might help him to get oriented a bit to see someone familiar.''

My knees felt wobbly with relief. "Yes, I would like to see him. Dan, do you want to go in, too? He'll be glad you got here. . . .''

Dan shook his head. "No. You can tell him. He doesn't need a lot of company right now, I wouldn't think. I'll stay here with Jill and Mickey.''

"Okay," I said, then spoke quickly to the doctor, who was already walking away. "Will he have to be here very long, do you think?''

"Overnight, anyway. Maybe a couple of days. We'll have to play that part of it by ear. He's going to be hurting quite a bit, so he might be more comfortable here where we can control the pain. Go on in, just keep it brief.''

I could hardly breathe as I walked into the cubicle where Sam lay on a high table in the middle of the room. A nurse smiled at me and said, "I'll be back in a minute.''

Sam looked chalky, and his eyes were glazed and unfocused. I cleared my throat and spoke softly.

"Sam? It's me. How do you feel?''

His tongue was thick. "Lisa? What happened?''

"Don't you remember? We hoped you'd be able to tell us.'' My heart was pounding. What if he had brain damage, after all? What if he didn't get his memory back?

"My head hurts. A ten-pound aspirin wouldn't cure my headache.'' He made an obvious effort to see me more clearly. "Did anyone else get hurt?''

"No, only you. You fell, out behind the stable.''

"Stable.'' He repeated the word vaguely as if it had no meaning to him.

I reached for his hand and squeezed it, but he didn't squeeze back.

"At Allendale, remember? You're caretaking at Allendale. Beau got here, he helped put you in the car and bring

60

you to the hospital. He's going to stay with us while you have to be here.''

"Beau. He's here?''

"He's outside in the waiting room. Do you want to see him?''

Sam's gaze drifted upward to the powerful light above him, puzzled. He moistened his lips. "Where am I?''

"In the hospital in Arlington. Do you want to see Beau?''

"No. It hurts too much to talk to anybody. Are they going to give me something for this headache?''

"I'm going to give you an injection,'' the nurse said, coming briskly through the doorway. She smiled at me. "Perhaps you'd better go now, miss.''

"Yes. All right. Don't worry, Sam, they're going to take good care of you. We'll be back to see you tomorrow and don't worry about Allendale. We'll hold the fort until you can come back.''

Sam made a guttural sound, deep in his throat, and closed his eyes. He didn't wince when the hypodermic needle sank into his hip or say good-bye.

I walked out of the E.R. with my eyes stinging. I wished Mom and Dad were here. I wished I'd found Sam yesterday. I wished we'd never gone near Allendale. And I hoped the doctor knew what he was talking about, that Sam wouldn't have any lasting damage.

Dan sprang up from one of the plastic chairs and crossed the room to meet me. "Did he tell you what happened?''

"No. He doesn't remember anything.'' It scared me to see Sam the way he was, in spite of the doctor's assurances.

"He probably will, once they set his arm and the concussion clears up,'' Dan soothed. "Come on, they'll take care of him. Let's go back to Allendale and make sure nothing's happening there that shouldn't be. We don't want Sam to lose his job because of this, do we?''

We went out into the bright sunshine. In the distance we

could see dark forested slopes of the Cascade foothills, with the snowy multiple peaks of Three Fingers beyond. Familiar, beautiful Washington countryside, the sight I'd grown up with. Familiar, yet different now.

I stumbled going off a curb and Dan grabbed my arm to steady me.

"What if Sam doesn't get his memory back?" I choked, and Dan tightened his grip.

"Hey, it'll come back," he said. "He knew who you were, didn't he? And he was hurting. You wait and see, by tomorrow he'll probably remember everything. The important thing is he's going to be okay."

We got into the station wagon in silence, and Dan drove us back. We were quiet to begin with, but by the time we reached the gates of the estate we were feeling better.

Dan told a funny story about having broken an ankle while skiing and all the things he'd done with his foot in a cast. No wonder Sam liked having him for a roommate; he was entertaining as well as attractive. Most people would have related such a mishap as a tragedy; Dan made it sound hilarious.

It didn't occur to me until the ignition had been turned off that in our haste to get Sam to a doctor, I'd forgotten to lock up the house.

I didn't say anything immediately because I was already feeling as if I'd been sufficiently stupid. But the minute I walked in the front door I stopped dead still.

"What's the matter?" Dan asked, pausing beside me, suddenly alert.

The hair had risen on the back of my neck. "I think . . . someone's been here while we were gone."

Jill and Mickey followed us inside and they, too, were tense.

"Why?" Dan asked. "What's different?"

"I don't know. . . ." I turned slowly in a circle, seeing nothing out of place. And then I realized what it was.

"Smell it? Tobacco smoke."

"I smell it, too," Jill confirmed. Her blue eyes were very wide.

"It didn't smell like this before." I was sure of that. "Nobody had been in the house in a long time, and it didn't really smell like anything except kind of stuffy."

"And there are no smokers in the crowd," Dan said softly. He turned around, gaze raking the big entryway, taking it for granted that it was true. "Let's see if we can follow the odor."

I wasn't sure I wanted to find anybody, but how could we possibly sleep tonight without knowing if the intruder was still here? "Maybe we ought to go back to town and tell the police," I said.

Dan sounded less apprehensive than I was. "Let's look around first, see if anything's been disturbed. The smell of tobacco will be long gone by the time the cops could get here."

It was gone faster than that. By the time we'd been in the house for a few minutes, going from room to room, we could no longer detect the tobacco smell. There was no way of knowing if the smoker had been in a particular part of the house or not, until Jill spoke in a peculiar voice.

"Wasn't that vase on the mantel?" she asked as we stood side by side in the doorway of the study.

Then I saw the broken remnants on the hearth and moved toward them as if drawn on an invisible string. "I don't remember where it was, but it wasn't broken on the floor. This is the kind of thing Sam was supposed to prevent. I wonder how valuable it was?"

"What did you find?" Dan came to join me, dropping to his knees and picking up one of the larger shards of painted china. "Oh, boy. It's an old one, Chinese, and definitely valuable. Maybe an expert could mend it, but I suppose the cracks would show where it was put back together."

"And that will reduce its value," I said dully. "It's not fair that Sam should be blamed for this, not under the circumstances." Especially, I thought, since I was the one who'd forgotten to lock up the house before we took Sam to the hospital. I felt like crying.

Jill's words came out in a squeaky way. "What if Sam didn't just fall out of the hayloft?"

"What do you mean?" I asked, even though I knew.

Sam had never been clumsy. He wouldn't have fallen out of the loft.

Which left only one conclusion, and as I looked into the faces of the others I knew we shared that knowledge.

Sam had been pushed, and then he'd been left there, maybe to die.

Dan had gathered up the remains of the broken vase and put them on the desk. "Maybe we better go check out the loft," he said.

Five minutes later I followed Dan up the wobbly ladder while Mickey and Jill waited below with anxious, upturned faces. Dust motes drifted in the shafts of sunlight that came through the places where shakes were missing on the roof, and there was the faint smell of old alfalfa hay.

And there was something else. I put out a hand to touch Dan's arm when I realized what it was.

"Dan," I whispered, and heard my voice quaver as fear swept over me.

8

Except for a single shaft of sunlight, the loft was dim, but there was no mistaking the smell of tobacco, and directly in the pool of light filtering through the hole in the roof was a cardboard box. I could see a jar of peanut butter, and when Dan and I stepped closer, we could see the other items as well.

Dan grunted, squatting beside the box. "Looks like some bum thought it was a good place to take shelter."

There was a rumpled roll of blankets in what remained of the hay, reeking of the tobacco odor we'd noticed in the house. There wasn't much more except part of a loaf of bread, several apples, and a couple of cans of pop in the box, and a man's shirt with a folded newspaper on it.

"He's living here," I said, glancing around now that my eyes had adjusted to the dimness to make sure the trespasser wasn't still here. "Sam must have surprised him—or the other way around. And he . . ."

I couldn't quite say it, so Dan did. "He could have shoved Sam out the loft door, all right. I wonder where he is now?"

"Let's get out of here," I suggested nervously. "It looks like he's been eating and sleeping here, and from the smell of his stuff I think he's the one who was in the house while we were gone."

Dan had picked up the newspaper. "My guess is that he

was in the house until you came," Dan said. "And then he moved out here."

"So he set a fire to drive us away that first night?" I said indignantly. "We could have been killed! And he was in the house again today while we were in town. He must have knocked that vase over and broken it, too. What for?"

Dan spoke absently, holding the newspaper so that the sunlight made it readable. "It's an old paper, but look at this."

I read aloud the first sentence of the article he was indicating. "Adam Allendale, prominent local citizen, died yesterday at the age of ninety-two." After that was an account of Mr. Allendale's accomplishments and philanthropies; the piece ended with, "He is survived by two grandsons, a granddaughter, and six great-grandchildren. See obituary, page 12."

Dan refolded the paper and dropped it where he had found it. He didn't seem as angry as I felt, but then he hadn't been in the caretaker's cottage when it was set on fire.

"So whoever's here knew Mr. Allendale died and the place was empty." I was thinking aloud. "Why would anyone come way out here in the country to hole up, though? He apparently doesn't have a car and it's a long way to town."

"Who knows?" Dan sounded speculative, as if he might have some private idea about that, but though I waited, he didn't say anything more. Instead, he walked beyond the trespasser's belongings and stood in the open doorway at the end of the barn, the one through which hay would have been lifted into the loft. The one through which Sam had probably fallen.

Or been pushed, I thought, rubbing my arms where the goose bumps had risen again.

"I think Sam came up here and found this stuff," I said. "And whoever it belongs to surprised him."

66

Dan nodded. "They argued, maybe. And he shoved Sam out the loft door. Yeah, it could have happened that way."

"Do you still think we shouldn't call the police? Or at least Mr. Allendale?"

Dan considered, though not for long. "It's Sam's decision, isn't it? We'll go back to the hospital tomorrow and see what he says. It can't make much difference to wait an extra day, not if we're safely locked up inside the house."

I was subdued as we descended the ladder and walked out of the dusky barn into brilliant sunlight. "It makes me uncomfortable to think about someone being on the grounds, someone with so little regard for anybody else's life. What if he decides to torch off the big house, too?"

"He won't," Dan said, with a conviction that startled me.

I paused, looking into his face. "How can you know that?"

Dan hesitated, then laughed ruefully. "I don't know. I just feel that maybe he's . . . looking for something in the house. He won't risk destroying it."

"What?" I was intrigued now, the fear fading since we were out in the open and there was no danger in evidence. "What makes you think that?"

He shrugged. "Because of that old newspaper he's kept, I guess. He read up on . . . the old man who died. If he were just a bum looking for shelter, why would he have kept that particular paper?"

I was only half-convinced. "What would he be looking for?"

"Any number of things. Mr. Allendale was an old man, eccentric from the sound of it. Look at what he contributed money to. A ministerial school, an organization for homeless dogs, a choral society, investigations of psychic phenomenon, research on some obscure disease he didn't have himself—"

"How do you know all that?" I interrupted. "It didn't say all that stuff."

"I read about him," Dan said, "in the newspapers. There's been a family fight over his money ever since the funeral. They named all the stuff he contributed to, which apparently made some members of his family think he was off his rocker. I'm only guessing, Lisa, but I'd bet anything this guy isn't going to try to burn down the big house. After all, he was probably living in the place until Sam arrived and drove him out into the barn. Listen, I've got a sleeping bag in the car, and a box of groceries. What say I take them inside and we put together a lunch?"

I looked at him thoughtfully as we reached the car he called "the silver streak" and he opened the door and hauled out a sleeping bag.

"You know, you're not quite what I thought you'd be like," I mused, accepting the bag.

He emerged from the car with a carton of groceries, grinning. "Oh, how am I different? What did good old Sam say about me?"

"Mostly he talked about your looks—and how many girls you had chasing after you."

Dan laughed. "So you pictured an old-fashioned gigolo? Hair greased down, looking through a monocle?"

"Well, not quite," I said, but I had to laugh, too. We started up the steps of the veranda. "Somehow you don't exactly fit the picture Sam painted."

I held open the door for him as we went into the house. "He didn't say anything about my brains? My mechanical ability?"

I couldn't tell from his face if he was joking or serious.

Now I was really uncomfortable. How could I tell him that I'd had the impression he got by largely on charm, that he wouldn't even have had passing grades if Sam hadn't coached him?

I couldn't say that he seemed much more friendly, less conceited than I'd expected. Or that I'd anticipated a rich spoiled-brat type who sort of took advantage of Sam's good nature.

It was true Dan drove a nice sports car, but it wasn't brand new; he wore ordinary jeans and Reeboks, just like Sam. He'd been helpful and really nice. But I couldn't say those things to a boy, could I? To a college man?

I dropped the sleeping bag at the foot of the stairs. "Sam's room's the first one on the right; you can share with Mick until Sam comes back, or choose another room. Jill and I have the first room on the left. Everything else is open, all two hundred bedrooms."

"As many as that?" Dan asked, amused. He headed for the kitchen with the box. I followed, hoping he'd drop the line I'd foolishly opened up.

Mickey was putting napkins and plates on the table while Jill mixed a bowl of tuna fish with chopped celery, onions, and mayonnaise for sandwiches. She gave us a shy smile.

"I hope this is all right. We were getting hungry."

"So were we," Dan assured her, putting the box on the counter. "Shall I just put this stuff away, and we'll use it when we need it? How about some of these with the sandwiches now?" He tossed an economy-size bag of potato chips onto the table, and Mickey eagerly ripped it open.

Dan stowed away his supplies as if he'd been familiar with the kitchen forever, dug into the freezer for ice cubes for soda, and crunched on a chip as he opened a jar of dill pickles.

Was that what being rich did for you? Assure your ease in any circumstances? I wondered. He hadn't brought only junk food, I noted, though to hear Sam tell it, you'd think he and his roommate lived on burgers, tacos, and pizza. There were brown bread and fresh fruit and vegetables as well as packaged rice and macaroni, so maybe even rich mothers talked nutrition to their kids.

He stared ruefully at a stack of TV dinners. "I forgot

about those when we found your brother. I think they're all defrosted. Do I dare refreeze them?''

"No," Jill and I said in a chorus. "We'll refrigerate them for now, and have them tonight," I added. "They're still ice cold, so they should be okay. This looks great, Jill. You're an expert with fruit salads. Come on, let's eat."

Jill went very still and Mickey's eyes grew large when we told them about the trespasser in the barn. "Are we going to call the police?" Jill asked softly.

It was Dan who answered in a decisive manner before I got my mouth open. "No, we'll wait until Sam's better before we do anything. It's his job that's on the line. He'll have to report to the Allendales, especially since an antique vase was broken, but they may not want to bring the police in. And maybe he won't lose the job if they don't know until he's ready to take over the responsibility again. In the meantime"—he paused to bite off a corner of his sandwich and chew it—"let's do a thorough search of this place."

Mickey's expression changed from apprehension to anticipation. "Yeah! What are we going to be looking for?"

"Anything out of place. Anything that might be hidden, which means we'll look in crevices and cracks, behind and under furniture. If it was only a tramp sleeping in the hayloft, he wouldn't break into the house and poke around unless it was to steal valuables. There's no sign he's done that—the silver and the art objects are still here. I think he's hunting for something. Maybe we can find it first."

Right then I had a crazy thought.

Dan sounded as if he knew more than the rest of us did. As if he guessed what we might be searching for. But how could he?

Yet when he felt me staring at him, his grin was so open, so friendly, so . . . yes, darn it, so charming, that whatever odd thing I'd felt melted away.

I was glad he was here. It would have been impossible to

70

remain here without Sam if Dan hadn't stayed, too. Sam and Dan had been roommates for a year, and I knew Sam trusted him.

Jill obviously had no doubts. She was watching Dan with a small smile. "When do we start? And how?"

"Right after we have some of that chocolate cake," Dan said, helping himself to another sandwich. "That is to be eaten, isn't it?"

"Sam said you were a chocolate lover," I remembered. "We've heard a lot about you, but we don't know what you've heard about us."

Dan considered. "Well, not much, actually. I know you're considered pretty decent—for a kid sister. Other than that— I guess I'll just have to find out for myself, won't I, and come up with my own opinions."

His smile suggested that he looked forward to it, which took away a little of my disappointment that Sam hadn't said anything nicer than that about me to him. I reached for the knife to cut the cake.

Ten minutes later, when we had gathered in the study as a starting place for the search, Dan explained what he had in mind.

He went to the desk and pulled out a drawer, turning it upside down after sorting through its contents. "Just check to see if anything's been fastened on the bottom of a drawer. Or hidden behind it." He dropped to his knees and peered into the empty space. "Or," he added when he stood up, "if there's a secret compartment in any of the furniture, or in the walls."

He reached out to rap with his knuckles on the paneling beside the desk.

Mickey was bug-eyed. "Wow! How will we know if there is one?" he demanded.

"It'll sound different. Hollow, instead of solid." Dan

71

moved to the fireplace and began the knuckle rapping at one side and then changed to the other.

Abruptly he stopped, then tapped again at a spot where he'd knocked before. "Listen! Doesn't that sound different?"

It did, though the difference was barely perceptible.

"Now what?" I asked. "Even if there's a hollow place, how do we—"

I never finished the sentence. A section of the paneled wall suddenly moved under Dan's fingers and slid to one side.

Again I had that peculiar feeling. What was he, a psychic? To walk right into this room and find a secret compartment in a matter of seconds?

We all surged forward to see what was in the opening behind the paneling.

"It's empty," Dan said, disappointment plain in both his face and his words. "Nothing there but dust."

"But it's a secret hiding place." Only Mickey was still enthusiastic. "And if there's one, there might be other ones, right? All we have to do is find them."

"Right," Dan said, trying to sound cheerful. "Keep looking."

My odd feeling wouldn't quite go away, but I went along with everybody else, tapping on walls, peeking under and behind the furniture, feeling like an idiot. Would Sam have thought this was productive, or would he have felt silly, too?

Ten minutes later Mickey's whoop of triumph brought us on the run to the library across the hall.

"Look what I found!" he shouted. "Is this what we're looking for?"

9

What Mickey eagerly extended for our inspection was a worn hundred-dollar bill.

"Where did you find it?" Jill breathed.

"I was looking for a secret panel at the end of the bookcase, the one on that wall. I saw this sticking out of the top of a book. Maybe there's money in all those books!"

I started to say that wasn't very likely, and then I saw Dan's face. He was gazing speculatively around the big library, at the thousands of books. Dan didn't think it was a crazy idea.

"It would take forever to find them, looking through one book at a time," Jill said slowly.

"It would if the money was put in helter-skelter," Dan agreed, walking to the nearest shelf and removing a book at random. He flipped rapidly through it, finding nothing. "Do you remember which book it came out of?"

"That one," Mickey said promptly. "The one that isn't pushed all the way back onto the shelf."

"*Treasures of America*." Dan read the title, then let the pages flop open. Another bill fluttered to the carpet.

Mickey scooped it up. "Hey, maybe there's a fortune hidden here! Are we going to look through every book?" It suddenly dawned on him what a job that would be and his face fell. "It would take the rest of the summer. We wouldn't even have time to swim."

Dan ran a hand along the shelf of books, speaking as if to himself. "There may be some kind of system—"

"What do you mean?" I asked, stepping closer to look over his shoulder.

"Unless he just used a bill for a bookmark, I wouldn't think he'd risk losing hundred-dollar bills by sticking them in any old book. The chances are nobody'd ever find them again unless he hid them systematically. Mr. Allendale had money, but I'd be surprised if he just threw it away. So if he wanted to hide it in his library, what kind of system would he work out?"

"Why would he hide it here instead of putting it in the bank?" Mickey wondered. He glanced at me. "I don't guess it's ours to keep, whatever we find. It belongs to Sam's boss, right?"

"To Mr. Allendale's heirs," Dan said. "People sometimes do funny things when they get old, Mick. Things that make sense to them but not to everybody else. People who remember the big Depression, before any of us were born, didn't always trust banks, because the banks failed then. They didn't give the money back to the ones who'd put it in there, and those people lost everything they had."

Jill nodded. "I remember my dad reading a story in the paper a few months ago about an old man who lived in a shack like a hermit and everybody thought he was a pauper because he went around taking food out of garbage cans. Only when he died they found over eighty thousand dollars hidden in a rip in his mattress. You think Mr. Allendale was like that? Hiding money around the house so he'd be able to get it when he needed it, without going to a bank?"

Dan was still inspecting the backs of books. "Hard to say. But if he did deliberately hide money here in the library, I'll bet he had some way of finding it again."

I looked at the book he still held. "Ones with red covers?"

"Could be," Dan said. "Let's try it."

74

"There's a whole row with red covers over there," Mickey pointed out, reaching for one of them. But there was nothing in it or in any of the other red ones.

"Here," Dan said, handing the last book to me. "Stick it back in there, will you?"

I took it, but instead of replacing it on the shelf I read the title aloud. "*Treasures of America*. Do you suppose the titles might be the clue?"

Dan gave me an approving glance. "Treasures, you mean? That's an idea. What else would mean treasures? Money?"

"How about *The Gold Country of California*?" Jill asked, reaching out for a book. "Gold is a treasure, isn't it? Oh!" She gave a cry of delight as several bills fell out when she opened the cover.

"Maybe you got it, Lisa," Dan said. "Let's find out, look for more titles with treasures or some kind of valuables in them!"

For the next hour we moved excitedly along the library shelves, taking down every book with a title that might be construed as referring to treasure or wealth.

At the end of that time, dusty and getting thirsty enough to head for the kitchen for cold drinks, I counted up the bills we'd found.

"There's over fourteen hundred dollars here," I said, "and we've hardly started on the books."

Mickey drooped over his root beer. "Are we going to have to spend the rest of our vacation looking for money that belongs to somebody else?"

I tended to share his feelings. It had been exciting to begin with, but it wasn't our money, and finding it wasn't solving our problems. "Let's tell Mr. Allendale about it and let him open a million books looking for the rest of it."

Dan laughed. "You're right. We won't get any of it, so why should we waste our time? I never figured cash is what the guy in the barn is looking for, though he'd probably take any he found."

"What do you think he's looking for?" I asked. Again I had that funny feeling about Dan's conviction that the intruder was searching for something. Sam and I weren't exactly stupid, and *we* hadn't figured out anything like that.

"Well, think in terms of a . . . a small packet, or an envelope. Something like that."

Mickey took one last slurpy pull on his straw. "Jewels?" he asked, reviving a little.

"Who knows? Maybe," Dan said, laughing again.

I didn't laugh. If Sam hadn't been hurt, he'd have been the one making the decisions, because it was his job. I wasn't sure about Dan totally taking charge, just because he was a male and a few years older.

How did he know there was something in this house to search for, something of more importance than all that money?

Maybe, I thought, Sam had known more than he'd told us. Had Mr. Allendale asked Sam to look for something that his grandfather might have hidden? If that were the case, it was reasonable that Sam might have told his roommate, though I sort of resented being left out of it. Why the secrecy?

By the following morning I was still trying to figure it out and not getting very far. It bothered me so much I almost didn't appreciate Jill's scrambled eggs, cocoa, and toast. It didn't seem to be dulling anybody else's appetite, though.

Beyond the windows, the pool sparkled enticingly in the sunlight. Dan drained his glass and stood up. "Let's take a break and swim before lunch," he suggested. "Then we can go back to searching."

Everybody except me made a general movement, but I stopped them. "Aren't we going to go in to the hospital? They might be releasing Sam today."

"Oh, yeah, sure. You kids want to go in by yourselves?"

Dan asked. He had his back to me, putting a glass in the dishwasher, and I couldn't see his face.

"We can't. Neither Jill nor I has a driver's license. We don't get driver's ed until second semester next year."

"Oh." Dan turned from the sink, smiling. "Okay. I just thought part of us could keep on looking around here. Do we all go in, or shall I go by myself, or what? I kind of hate to go off and leave the place empty. I don't suppose anyone but me wants to stay here alone."

He had that right, but we had to check on Sam. And my uneasiness about Dan was growing, though I still didn't quite know why.

"You think whoever's sleeping in the barn will try to get in here again?" I asked, and Dan didn't hesitate.

"Sure, don't you? I mean, if he'd found what he wanted here, he'd have taken his stuff out of the loft and moved on by now. So yes, I think he'll try again. Even having the place locked wouldn't guarantee he couldn't get in. After all, he could just break a window if there's no one around to hear it."

"I don't want to swim," I said, for the first time crossing whatever Dan had said. "I think we should just go see Sam. After all, he's not getting paid to stand up against a criminal, is he? And we're not getting paid at all, so why should we take risks? Sam only talked about keeping vandals away. Kids, not men. The doctor thought he'd be fully conscious today, and he can decide if he even wants to keep the job under the circumstances."

It sounded reasonable to me. Dan didn't knuckle under, though. "And what if Sam's upset because we left the place unguarded? I mean, the guy's been sneaky, he'd not likely to break in if he knows somebody's still here. Why don't I go to town by myself, and you can lock yourselves inside if you want to, and we'll see what Sam says."

I wasn't exactly thrilled with his idea, but I supposed he

77

had a point. Besides, he didn't owe us anything. We couldn't make him stay here with us. Reluctantly, I agreed then; Dan would check with Sam, we'd hold the fort.

"It won't take me long," Dan said encouragingly. "I should be back in an hour."

Mickey was getting himself some chips, apparently not caring one way or the other as long as we didn't leave him by himself. I thought Jill felt the same way I did, from the look on her face, but she was willing to do whatever the rest of us decided.

"You can play music, nice and loud, so any prowler will know the place isn't empty," Dan pointed out. "And the station wagon's here. It'll only take a few minutes to talk to Sam, and I'll be right back, okay?"

It wasn't until Dan had gone that it occurred to me that if playing loud music gave warning to an intruder, it would also mask the noises that intruder might make, getting inside. Anything short of breaking glass, and what could we do if we heard that?

By then it was too late to reconsider. I stared at Jill and recognized the same fear that I felt myself.

We were alone again, and we didn't like it.

10

The house seemed strangely enlarged and empty. Dan was hardly out of sight before I was wishing we'd gone with him, even if someone carried away the entire place while we were gone.

"Maybe it's silly to stay behind locked doors in broad daylight this way, but I'll feel better if we do," I muttered.

Mickey stared out the window at the pool glinting in the sunlight. "Geez, Lisa, am I going to have to stay locked up inside the rest of the time we're here?"

Jill and I exchanged looks and I cleared my throat. "I'd feel better if you didn't go outside today, Mick. At least not until Dan comes back. We don't really know why that tramp is living in the hayloft, but since Sam got hurt out there, it doesn't seem like a good idea to run around alone. It won't be for long." I hoped, I thought, crossing my fingers.

Mickey scowled. "So what'm I s'posed to do? I'm tired of opening up books looking for money that isn't even mine when I find it."

"Me too," I admitted.

"We've explored the three main floors of the house," Jill said tentatively, "but we haven't been in the attic. Why don't we see what's up there? Sometimes there's fascinating stuff in old attics."

Mickey didn't quite cheer up. "Okay. Let's see the attic. It better be interesting, though."

"Nobody's been up here in a long time," I said, sneezing from the dust as I started upward on the final flight of stairs. "So why is the hair prickling on my arms?"

There was nobody in the attic. It was huge and crammed with odds and ends.

"What a bunch of junk," Mickey said, disappointed.

"We haven't even looked around yet," I said. "Look, there's a spinning wheel. I'll bet it's an antique."

My little brother wasn't interested in a spinning wheel or in a box of tarnished silver that Jill tripped over or in rocking chairs, chamber pots, and outdated calendars, though Jill and I paused to look at them all.

"Hey, now this is more like it!" Mickey said suddenly, and I turned to see what he'd found.

"Look! It's an electric train and see what goes with it!"

Jill put down a picture she was examining, and I turned away from the intricately carved dresser that must have taken several strong men to get up here.

"Oh, look," Jill said, "there's a whole village! What a pretty little church, and there's the depot—"

"And track," Mickey said with satisfaction. "Tons of track. More even than Jimmy Peluso has. Let's take it all downstairs so we can plug it in and see if it still runs."

I hesitated, looking at Jill. "The Allendales might not like it if we mess around with their stuff."

"I won't break anything," Mickey promised. "Look, there's a sawmill—I think the saws move when you plug it in!"

"I always thought it would be fun to have something like this," Jill said, and the wistfulness in her voice won me over. It *did* look like fun, especially when we had to stay inside for a while.

"Well, okay. Be careful with it, though. Maybe you can set it up in the front hallway. The floor isn't carpeted, and there's plenty of space. Jill and I are going to look around here for a while," I told him.

He couldn't have been more than halfway down the top flight of stairs when there was a crash, and then before I could yell Mickey shouted, "It's okay, nothing broke!"

I sighed and hoped Sam wouldn't be mad about him taking the stuff downstairs. Mick needed something to do to keep him from going crazy. For that matter, so did I.

Jill had opened up a trunk and in the dim light through the dirty windows I saw that she'd lifted out a crimson satin evening gown. She turned to me with a delighted grin. "Wouldn't this have been fun to play with when you were dressing up in your mother's old clothes?"

"Mom had a fancy dress I used to borrow when she didn't wear it anymore. All lace and ruffles. Once we put on a play, when we were about eight or nine years old, and we pretended we were princesses. I wore Mom's pale pink, and Marcia wore a gold brocade."

How long would it be before I stopped getting a lump in my throat every time I thought about Marcia? I guess something showed in my voice, because Jill spoke uncertainly.

"Marcia's your best friend."

"She was," I said. "I suppose you heard about us. What happened just before you moved to Granite."

She shook her head. "No. Nobody really talked to me until you did."

And I probably wouldn't have talked to a newcomer if my old gang had still been my friends. Now it was my turn to blush, and I hoped she didn't notice.

"Well, you must be the only kid in school who doesn't know. Sam says I should just forget about it, but it still hurts, what she did."

"I'm sorry," Jill said softly, and I thought she really was.

"Everybody else has dumped me. I may not have done

81

you a favor by making friends with you. A lot of people think I'm a thief and a cheat, I guess."

She looked so troubled—and on my behalf, I thought, not her own—that I felt compelled to go on.

"We had an important exam coming up, and Marcia'd been goofing around with Paul Pittman instead of studying. She never confided in me, so I don't know exactly how she got hold of the test answers sheet, but she helped out in the school office sometimes. I suppose she saw it there somewhere and took it. Anyway, Miss Albers found it in our locker, Marcia's and mine."

Jill waited, biting her lip.

"I don't know why she looked there, even, except that we both got good grades on the tests. So did a few other people. Maybe Miss Albers realized one of the answer sheets was missing, and she was checking all kinds of places. Anyway, she found the answer sheet, and they called both of us into the office to ask about it."

The humiliation of that moment still made me feel sick.

"I told the truth, that I'd never seen the sheet before. I knew Marcia must have had it—nobody else could get into our locker—and I couldn't believe it when Marcia swore she'd never seen it before, either."

"She lied about it," Jill murmured.

"Yes. I could tell by her face she was lying, but nobody else seemed to be able to. They made us all take the test again, the whole class, only it was a different one. So everybody was mad about that, all the ones who hadn't cheated."

I could close my eyes and see their faces, the angry students who resented repeating a difficult test. I could remember their comments about it, too.

My eyes stung now as they had then. "It seemed like everybody believed Marcia, not me. A lot of them made crummy remarks to me, anyway."

"But couldn't they tell, when you retook the test . . . ?"

What was intended to be a laugh came out more like a sob. "That was part of the problem. Nobody but Bill Wilson got a really good grade the second time. I was so upset after what they'd said to me just beforehand—accused me of—that I couldn't think straight. I passed, and so did Marcia, but not with the grades we'd had the first time around. Anyway, Sam said I was better off without Marcia leading me around by the nose, and that it was my imagination that everybody else avoided me. It wasn't, though. All my so-called friends sided with Marcia. If you hadn't moved to town, I don't think anybody would have been talking to me."

Behind me, Mickey was clattering up the stairs for another load of railroad tracks. "Hey, Lisa, when you come, bring that last box, will you?" he requested, and probably didn't even hear my answer before he was tearing back down.

I was glad the interruption had ended the subject I was sorry to have brought up. I reached into the trunk and held up a dress. "Can you imagine wearing this?"

Jill laughed, and the moment passed.

We pawed through a lot of junk, but the only thing I found that was really interesting was a box of photo albums. "I think I'll take these downstairs," I said. "I'm curious about the people who lived here. Sometimes I feel as if the family is still here, sort of ghostly figures that float just out of my line of vision, about to pick up a basket of knitting or the pipe on the table in the study, or the book left open in the library."

I laughed self-consciously. "It's as if, if I turned suddenly, I'd catch them." It was the kind of remark Marcia would have though absurd, and then I'd have pretended I was kidding.

Jill, however, replied thoughtfully. "I know what you mean. Allendales lived in this house for almost a hundred years—there's a date scratched in the cement of the foundation at the back of the house. My grandmother says the inhabitants leave an impression on a house, even after they're gone.''

"Really?" I felt a sudden rush of gratitude toward Jill's grandmother. And toward Jill herself, I decided, and picked up the photograph albums. Just as we reached the hall at the bottom of the attic stairs we heard the unmistakable sound of smashing glass. A lot of it.

I clutched the albums against my chest and ran toward the front stairs. "Mickey?"

There was no answer, and I pounded down the stairs, Jill right behind me.

Mickey wasn't killed anyway, though his freckles stood out like paint spatters on pale cheeks; he stood in the midst of train and track parts scattered over the entryway.

"What happened?" I demanded, breathless.

"I don't know. I was afraid to go look," Mickey confessed. "I think somebody broke in."

"Which direction did it come from?" I dropped the albums on a low table, my heart thumping like mad. Why hadn't we all gone to town with Dan and let the house take care of itself?

Mickey pointed. "I think it was back there somewhere. Maybe in the kitchen."

I glanced at Jill, who was pale, too. "Do we go back and look? Or go outside and wait for Dan to come back?"

Jill licked her lips. "We were locked inside. If there's someone in here with us—"

I swallowed. "If it's kids, they may have scared themselves off, making so much noise." There was no noise now. "Come on. Let's go together and see."

The house was perfectly normal. No broken windows, nothing out of the ordinary at all.

We hadn't imagined that horrendous crash, I thought, hoping that if anyone was somewhere ahead of us they'd leave

84

before we got there. "Something smashed, something big. We ought to be able to find it."

We went through the house, one room at a time. An intruder would hear us breathing, maybe even hear our hearts pounding. Mine sounded like a tom-tom.

And then we reached the dining room and there it was.

I drew in a ragged breath, and Jill moaned. "Oh, no! I'll bet it was worth a fortune!"

Mickey ducked his head under my elbow to see, too. "Oh, wow! No wonder it made such a racket!"

The crystal chandelier over the long table had been magnificent. Jill had turned it on our first evening in the house, just to see what it looked like all lit up.

Now it lay on the table, having gouged deeply into the wooden surface, the crystals splintered and crushed. Bits of cut glass were sprinkled over the floor, glinting diamondlike over the deep blue carpet.

I felt sick. Would Sam somehow be blamed for this? "How could it have come down? It must have been there for years, so why did it suddenly fall?"

Jill sounded hollow. "I don't think it did," she said.

"What do you mean?" My legs felt shaky, and I wanted to sit down.

Jill stretched out a hand to the wall beside her. "See this hook? And the cord? It's used to raise and lower the chandelier so it can be cleaned, or the bulbs changed. We lived in Savannah once for six months, and a girlfriend and I went through some of the old historic houses. Several of them had marvelous chandeliers like this one. Originally most of them held candles; the flames were reflected in all the crystal to magnify the light. Later they were wired for electricity. Once or twice a year they'd take the fixture down to clean all those little pieces of crystal, and this is how they did it. All that glass is very heavy, and the chandelier I remember best took two men to lower it or pull it back up. If one person tried to lower it by himself, it would probably have fallen unless he was very strong."

I stared at the cord, no longer secured around its hook, and then at the mess on the table. "You think that's what happened? Somebody tried to bring the chandelier down and lost control, so it fell?"

"I noticed the cord the other day when I turned on the light," Jill said. "There was dust on the knots holding it in place. It hadn't been touched in ages, probably not since they closed up the house. It was securely fastened, and the cord hasn't been cut. Someone just about had to have slipped it off the hook."

I was confused and scared. "It's nuts. Who did it? How did they get in?" And where were they now? That might be even more important than what I'd said aloud.

Jill had as many questions as I did. "And why did they lower the chandelier? Was it to make a crash and scare us? Or was it an accident?"

"Maybe there was something hidden in it," Mickey suggested, heading toward the table and the smashed crystal.

"Mick, no, don't touch anything," I said quickly.

"I just want to see if there's anyplace something could have been hidden," Mickey protested as I held him back. "This is such a crazy place. Maybe there was money in the lights, too."

"Maybe. I guess something small could have been stuck in that fancy silvery part. But we're not going to touch it. We'll have to report this to the Allendales, and it'll be best if they see it just the way it is now. Come on, let's see if any of the doors or windows are unlocked."

"Wait," Jill said suddenly. My heart had just started slowing down and now it began hammering all over again when she asked, "What's this?"

She stooped to pick up a crumpled paper from the under one of the chairs. "This could have been in the chandelier, maybe in that metal bracket.'' She smoothed the paper flat and held it so that I could read it, too.

Disappointment made my voice flat. "It's nothing important. Just a date.''

"A date almost a year ago,'' Jill agreed. "It could be when they last cleaned the chandelier, the way they did it in a house in Savannah. Someone''—she swallowed and glanced around—"could have seen the paper and brought the chandelier down, thinking it was something important hidden there. Then he wadded it up and dropped it when he found out it didn't mean anything.''

It seemed logical, only I didn't care anymore. I just wanted not to be scared. "Let's see if we can find how somebody got in here,'' I said. "And then when Dan comes back, no matter what Sam's decided, we're getting out. Dan can take us home.''

It was spooky, trekking from room to room to inspect windows and doors. We felt like someone might jump out at us any minute.

Nothing happened, though. There were no signs of breaking and entering, no unlocked doors. We were sitting on the front steps, waiting, when the silver streak got back.

Dan didn't give us a chance to speak first, and his face was so sober I jumped up in alarm. "Is Sam worse? What did he say?''

"I didn't get to see Sam,'' he said. "They were getting him ready to take by ambulance to Harborview.''

That's a hospital in Seattle, one where they handle trauma patients. I grabbed his arm, forgetting to breathe.

"No, Lisa, don't panic! He's no worse, but they're concerned about his head injury and they want him to be seen by a specialist and have some tests. They don't have the equipment to do them in Arlington. They said he'll probably be there for a day or so.''

"But they wouldn't do that if it wasn't serious, would they?"

"Well, they don't think it's anything critical. They're just playing it safe by having this specialist see him. If it does turn out they have to do surgery, they'll have to get hold of your folks, the doctor said. They wouldn't want to do anything like that with just the paper they signed before they left—"

I was suffocating. "Are you talking about brain surgery?"

He put his hand over mine. "I'm sorry you weren't there to talk to the doctor, because it wouldn't frighten you so much if you heard the way they put it. It's a precaution, not an emergency. Honest. I'm concerned about Sam, too, but there's no reason to freak out. They said we could check back at Arlington tomorrow and they'd be able to give us a report. Can you locate your folks if they need them?"

I scarcely heard him. I felt numb with anguish and guilt. Dan was still talking, but I'd forgotten about demanding to be taken home at once.

"Come on, I brought back burgers and fries from Rotten Ralph's, so let's eat while it's still hot. Then we'll talk about the situation."

I let him steer me inside, where Dan stopped at the sight of the miniature village and the train tracks all over the floor. "Hey, neat! Where did this come from?"

"The attic," Mickey said. "I won't hurt it. It's a neat train set. I'm hungry, and I can smell those burgers. Let's eat."

It wasn't until Jill and I were cleaning up the kitchen that I remembered we'd brought something else down from the attic.

"Hey, let's look at those photographs we found upstairs," I said, and Jill turned on the dishwasher and followed me toward the front of the house where the boys had gone.

But there was nothing on the table at the foot of the stairs when we got there.

The photograph albums had disappeared, and they were nowhere to be found.

11

Mickey was indignant. "Why would I take a bunch of old pictures of people I don't even know?" he demanded. "Don't blame me if they're gone."

I believed him. Mickey was a pest sometimes, but he wasn't a liar. "Then where did they go?" I asked, but the only response was troubled faces.

"It's been a rough day," Dan said, sighing.

"You don't even know the worst of it yet," I told him. "Look in the dining room."

He wasn't prepared for the damage there. I couldn't blame him for swearing under his breath. He listened to Jill's explanation of how the chandelier could be lowered and agreed that probably someone had tried to do it and dropped it because it was too heavy. Then he looked at me.

"It must have made a heck of a crash. Maybe you left the albums somewhere else, Lisa. You were upset when you came downstairs after hearing that, and afraid of what had happened. We'll probably find the pictures somewhere else."

I stared into his eyes. "I put them on the lamp table at the foot of the stairs. I remember distinctly."

Nobody said anything, and I suddenly recalled how it had felt to be under suspicion myself.

"I'm not accusing any of you," I said lamely. "I thought we'd managed to lock that creep out of the house, but *he* must be the one who took them. I can't imagine why, though.

90

And when the owners find out what's been happening, they'll fire Sam."

I gulped, and my throat stung. "They may even hold him responsible for that vase that got broken. It makes me sick to think about the chandelier, too. What do you suppose it cost?"

I guess I sounded as near to tears as I was, and Dan gave me a look that was more sympathetic. "A lot, but they surely have insurance to cover it, the same as they do for the fire. It wasn't Sam's fault, either the fire or the chandelier breaking."

"But he's supposed to be keeping vandalism from happening! It wasn't fair to expect him to deal with this kind of thing; it's been far worse than kids fooling around! That's no kid staying out in the barn, and I don't think it was a kid who set fire to the cottage, either. Sam's been hurt, maybe seriously, and we can't wait any longer to report to the Allendales and tell them to find someone else or call the cops, because we're leaving."

Dan's voice was gentle. "Look. Within a day or so we'll know for sure how Sam is and be able to talk to him and see what he wants you to do. I'll bet he doesn't want to lose this job, and he deserves the chance to explain to Mr. Allendale himself about what's happened. I'll be here until Sam's back," he said. "You won't be alone. You're shivering—are you cold?"

"No." I blurted the truth. "I'm scared of staying in this house, even with you here!"

He talked some more about how the decisions to be made were really up to Sam, and how another night here wasn't going to make that much difference, that nothing more was going to happen.

I didn't see how he could be sure of that, but somehow I let him convince me. Jill kept looking at me, not saying anything, though I thought she was pretty nervous, too. Dan finally talked us around because he was so calm about it. Probably the way Sam would have been if he'd been there.

Once more we checked the doors and windows without finding any of them unlocked. Dan didn't say so, but I had the idea he didn't believe Jill's theory about how the chandelier had fallen but thought it had simply been an accident.

"Hey, let's help Mickey put this train set together," he said, and for a while we entertained ourselves that way and gradually forgot to worry about our strange situation.

When Dan got tired of the trains and went upstairs to look around again, Jill and I gave up any pretense of interest in the trains, too, and sat on the stairs, talking quietly.

"I don't feel like I can let him out of my sight," I said, envying Mickey his ability to forget reality and enjoy the miniature cars and engines. "This is turning out to be some crummy vacation for you, Jill. I'm sorry."

"It's not your fault. I just hope Sam's all right."

"Me too. I don't know how I'll face Mom and Dad if he isn't. It might have made a difference if I had found him sooner—"

"That wasn't your fault, either. You went around the barn, calling him. How could you know he was unconscious?"

"I wish my folks weren't going to tour Europe after Dad's conference is over. I don't know how Dad would feel about Sam staying here, but I'm pretty sure Mom would want us to go home and let the Allendales get someone else who's a real security guard."

Jill spoke hesitantly. "I suppose we can't go into Seattle to see Sam?"

"Not unless Dan takes us, and he's made it pretty clear he thinks it's a stupid idea when Sam is supposed to be back in Arlington so soon. It would mean being away for at least three or four hours, and I almost think I'd be scared to come back in here after that much time. Who knows? Whoever's prowling around could set booby traps all over the place or something.''

"I've got a hunch my dad would feel the same way as your mom. That we ought to get out.''

I straightened hopefully. "Maybe we ought to call him and tell him what's going on, see what he says.'' That would take the decision away from Dan, or me.

The familiar flush traveled up her throat into her face. "We can't get him. He's gone down to Vancouver to see about a job, remember?''

"Oh, I forgot. Does that mean if he gets the job you'll have to move again?''

"I don't know. He *has* a job, but it doesn't pay very well, and he needs a better one.''

"Well, if it's just for a job interview, he won't be gone long, will he? We'll call him when he gets home.''

Jill's color was warmer than ever. Imagine being that insecure about talking to a friend, even a new one, I thought. "We don't have a phone,'' Jill said.

"Oh, they haven't put it in yet? I didn't realize it would take so long to get one, unless you have to wait for a private line. Well, let's talk about something else. What'll we have for supper?''

The afternoon passed slowly. Dan came down around three, wiping dust off his hands onto his jeans. "Anybody want to go swimming?'' he asked. "It's getting hot upstairs.''

Mickey didn't want to leave the trains—the setup covered almost the entire spacious entryway now—and I refused to leave him alone in the house. It wound up with me sitting there feeling sorry for myself while Jill and Dan were out in the pool, though Jill had offered to stay with me if I wanted her to.

I did, but I couldn't say so without sounding as rotten as I was feeling.

Nobody talked much during our salad and fried-chicken dinner, and when Dan suggested listening to music afterward, I shrugged. I'd made up my mind to *demand* that Dan take us back to Granite Falls to consult Jill's dad when he came home day after tomorrow, unless we'd talked to Sam before then.

Mickey refused to go up to bed alone, and I didn't argue. I didn't want to be on the second floor by myself, either.

Finally, at only about nine o'clock, Dan stood up and stretched. "Guess I'll take one last tour of the ground floor, check the windows and doors. Then I'm going to turn in and read for a while."

So we all went up early. I laid out my clothes for the next day on a chair and started to undress. Jill glanced at my clean shorts and shirt and underwear questioningly.

I felt both silly and defiant. "Just in case I need to get dressed in a hurry in the middle of the night," I said.

Marcia would probably have hooted at me. Jill nodded thoughtfully and put out her own set of clothes, including a pale blue knit shirt with a white diagonal stripe across the front of it.

"I like your shirt," I told her, pulling on my pajamas. "Marcia used to have one just like it. She was practically sick when some idiot at a picnic waved a cigarette around and burned a hole in it. It was brand new, almost."

Jill had her back to me. She jerked, then bent forward, muttering. "Darned button just popped off. Where did it go?"

She finally found it, under the dresser, and joined me in our sleeping bags on the bed. "I hope we don't need those clothes in a hurry, in the middle of the night."

She said it lightly, but I knew she meant it, the same as I did.

It took quite a while to fall asleep. I don't know how much later it was that I woke up, chilled. I pulled the top flap of

94

my sleeping bag up over me, shivering. Had I heard something? Mickey having a bad dream, maybe? I thought maybe I'd had one of my own, but I couldn't remember what it had been about.

I snuggled down into the warmth and had almost drifted off again when I heard something for sure.

My grandparents' house is old, and sometimes it creaks at night. Sam used to scare me with tales about ghosts when I was little, until I woke up screaming once and Mom bawled him out.

This was an old house, too, and I no longer believed in ghosts. But after what had already happened here, I listened intently. Had I heard a door close?

Jill was asleep beside me. Maybe Mickey or Dan, going to the bathroom?

There was another sound: a board creaked. Not close by, but some distance away.

I waited, but there was nothing more. I didn't hear running water or anybody going back to bed. It was probably just the old wood, expanding or contracting, whichever it did at night. The sensible thing was to go back to sleep.

Except that I couldn't.

The next noise, which I'd never have heard if I hadn't been holding my breath, was different. Like the sound we'd made in the attic when we shoved a heavy dresser to one side to get at the last box of train tracks.

I felt a spurt of anger at Sam, that he was miles away in a hospital when he should have been here with us. Or should have taken us home by this time. Dan was across the hall, only a few yards away, but he wasn't Sam. Would he make fun of me if I woke him up?

I was wide-awake now, and when it came again I was positive. Someone was moving around the house in the darkness.

I could stay here shivering and scaring myself, I thought,

or I could get up and find out what was going on. I swallowed hard and threw aside the top layer of the sleeping bag.

In bare feet I padded toward the door, flashlight clutched in one hand. I'd have liked the electric lights, but if it turned out to be a branch brushing a window, I didn't want to be ridiculed about it for the rest of my life.

I paused in the second-floor hallway to listen again. Nothing.

Taking a breath, I turned on the flashlight. The hall was empty, just the way it ought to be. The nearest bathroom door was open, the room dark.

Across the hall the boys' door was open, too. I kept the light low, swinging it to see that Mickey was sprawled on the floor, mostly out of his sleeping bag. The covers were mounded in the shadows on the bed beside him, and I turned away. I wasn't ready to wake Dan up.

I wished I could convince myself that whatever I'd heard was harmless. Maybe I could if I worked harder at it.

And then it came again, the sound like heavy furniture being slid across a wood floor.

I was cold, and I wished I had a bathrobe. Mom said we lived in Washington State because she liked the way it got cool at night, so you could sleep, no matter how hot it was in the daytime. Right then I'd rather have been warm than in a cold sweat.

What was I going to do? Search the whole second floor by myself? Or stand here all night? I didn't have a clue where to begin, and I was practically spooked out of my mind.

There was a subdued thud. It came from somewhere down the dark hall. Not the wind blowing a branch against the house. Not a mouse in the walls.

My chest hurt, and I sucked in a deliberate breath. I didn't want to move, but somehow my feet were taking me forward, step by cautious step.

And then I saw it. Pencil thin, a line of light under one of the bedroom doors.

For long seconds I stared at it. I don't know where the courage came from then; maybe I was just furious at whoever was scaring us witless, too angry to have any sense. Anyway, I reached out for the knob and twisted it before I lost my nerve.

12

The knob turned without a sound and the door opened inwardly. This wasn't one of the rooms where we'd removed the protective sheeting; a massive four-poster bed loomed like the ghost of some great monster straight ahead of me.

There was other sheeted furniture, too. The exception was a tall chest. It had not only been uncovered, it had been moved; there were scratches on the waxed floor and an outline on the wallpaper where the chest had stood.

I don't know what I expected to find here, but it certainly wasn't a tall familiar figure in jeans and a blue knit shirt.

"Dan!" I blurted, and he swung around to face me, startled.

For a moment the blue eyes were almost hostile, the nostrils flared, and then Dan relaxed. "You scared me to death," he said.

"What do you think you did to me?" I demanded, as much angry at what I'd just been through as relieved to find that it wasn't the cigarette-smoking intruder. "What are you doing in here?"

"I couldn't sleep. Kept thinking about everything—what might be hidden that someone's searching for. So finally I got up and decided to look around some more."

I stared at him resentfully. "It never occurred to you that we might hear you and think it was the guy who's living in the barn?"

"I thought I was being quiet enough so you wouldn't hear me."

"I heard you." I almost choked on the words. "I was terrified."

"But you came to investigate." He smiled approvingly. "I knew you were a gutsy girl."

I was still shaking and icy cold. Another time I might have felt complimented, but not now. "Don't patronize me," I snapped, and the smile slid off his face. "Why are you moving furniture around in the middle of the night?"

"To see what's behind it."

I stared at the unfaded rectangle of wallpaper where the chest had stood. "And what was?"

"Nothing," Dan said smoothly. "But you never know until you look, do you? I'm sorry, I never meant to wake anybody. Come on, let's go back to bed. I didn't find a thing."

I didn't move. "Aren't you going to move the chest back where it belongs?"

"In the morning. No sense waking up everybody else." He came toward me and put a hand on my arm. "I really am sorry, Lisa. Forgive me?"

I didn't answer. He withdrew his hand after a moment and headed for the door, but before he could turn off the light I stopped him.

"Why did you pick this room to prowl around in?"

"I think it's the master bedroom. You know, where old Mr. Allendale spent his last weeks before he died. If he hid something, maybe it's here rather than downstairs. I thought I'd look, anyway."

He flicked the switch, and we were back to depending on my flashlight as we headed toward the front of the house. The swinging light made shadows leap and dart around us.

"How do you know that was Mr. Allendale's room?"

"I found a lot of stuff I figured belonged to him. On the dresser, on the nightstand."

"They were all covered up with sheets." I was amazed at how suspicious I sounded. This was Sam's buddy, Beau, and my brother would have been annoyed at how rude I sounded.

Beau—or Dan—replied patiently enough. "I lifted the sheets and looked, then put them back. Lisa, I can see that hearing me really upset you, and I understand why. I'm sorry."

He'd apologized twice. What could I do but accept that and go back to sleep for whatever was left of the night?

That was easier said than done. Jill slept peacefully, but it took me a while to warm up and even then I was so overloaded with adrenaline I couldn't sleep.

I didn't like the thoughts that were running through my head. Dan had been poking around upstairs while the rest of us were setting up the train. Why hadn't he investigated Mr. Allendale's room then, instead of in the middle of the night? Did he expect to find something he didn't want the rest of us to know about?

I knew that was stupid, but my head wouldn't shut off. Why was he convinced that the intruder was looking for something specific? Why did he think there was something to look for in the first place? He said he'd read about Mr. Allendale in the paper. Was there something valuable missing, something important? But if that were the case, the Allendales themselves would surely have searched thoroughly for it after the old man died.

I was glad Dan was here—the rest of us would never have dared stay here without him—but even though I knew he had a reputation of being kind of gung-ho with fleeting enthusiasms, I thought he was overdoing it this time.

He had a reputation with girls, too, but I wouldn't have thought very many of them would have liked being patronized. A gutsy girl, indeed. As if girls were mostly less gutsy than guys. That still rankled.

I finally drifted back into sleep and disturbing dreams I could barely remember when morning came, dreams about sinister forces and lurking figures in the shadows. I woke up tired and grouchy.

Everybody else had already dressed and gone downstairs, I discovered, chagrined. They hadn't been too far ahead of me, though. Jill was making waffles in that fancy Belgian waffle maker we'd discovered yesterday, and there was the smell of sausage.

Jill smiled a greeting, and Dan waved a hand, as if we'd parted last night on the best of terms. He was rummaging in the refrigerator.

"The orange juice is buried behind about two cases of root beer. Who the heck drinks that much of it? Nobody likes Pepsi but me? Or 7UP?"

"Sam's a root-beer freak, remember? He even drinks it for breakfast sometimes," I said, opening a cupboard. "Here's a pitcher for the juice. I'll set the table."

"Oh, yeah, I forgot. Where's a can opener for the juice?" He measured out water to dilute it. "You'll see that I'm very handy in the kitchen."

"Commendable, I'm sure. You didn't catch that from Sam; the best he can do is pop the top on a root-beer can."

"Oh, my mom insisted a boy needed to learn to do kitchen chores. After my sister screamed because I got off with no more than mowing the grass and taking out the garbage while she had to do dishes and set tables and learn to cook."

Jill was busy with the waffles, so I started turning sausages. "I didn't know you had a sister. I always had the impression you were an only child."

Dan paused, then stirred the juice more vigorously.

"Oh, technically I guess I am. I have a stepsister, though. Patty. She's fifteen. Shall we use big glasses, or little ones?"

While we ate the waffles and sausages, everybody else talked while I sat in silence. I don't even know what they talked about. I was engrossed in my own thoughts, and I didn't like them.

How, I wondered, could anyone have been Sam's roommate for a whole year and not have known Sam was addicted to root beer? He was a real pain about it, actually.

And there was that candy wrapper we'd found in the barn. Everybody who knew Sam knew he loved chocolate, but refused to eat it if you put nuts or raisins in it.

Maybe it was possible that Dan was so wrapped up with girls that he didn't pay any attention to what a roommate did, but it seemed very strange to me. Sam was never shy about letting his likes and dislikes be known.

And there was the matter of Dan's stepsister. I was positive Sam had said Beau was an only child, and kind of spoiled. Why would he have failed to mention a stepsister?

Confused and uneasy, I let the rest of them clear away after breakfast, excusing myself with no explanation. I climbed the stairs and went straight to the room where I'd found Dan last night, not sure what I was looking for but compelled to do something.

Dan was right about Mr. Allendale's belongings. I lifted sheet corners and found various items like monogrammed brushes and an old-fashioned wedding picture and a pipe stand.

Dan had said he'd move the dresser back where it belonged; so far he hadn't done it. I pushed tentatively on the chest, to see if I could return it to its original place. It was heavy and resisted my first effort. When I threw all my weight into it, though, it slid with the protesting sound I'd heard in the middle of the night.

I almost missed what the displaced chest had hidden.

I'd thrown one of the dustcovers over it, only to have it slide off, and I bent down to get it. The chest didn't quite cover the unfaded part of the wallpaper, so I'd have to shove it one more time.

There was wainscoting below the wallpaper, and there was a crack in that wooden paneling. Even then it didn't register until I'd pushed the chest once more and overshot the mark. And then I saw the crack on *that* side.

I hesitated, letting my gaze follow the cracks up to where they disappeared behind a picture of a woodland scene.

Cracks, about two and a half feet apart. Not just in the wooden panels, but in the wallpaper, too. When the high chest was in place, they wouldn't be visible.

The barely visible cracks disappeared behind the painting. I used both hands to lift it down from the wall and knew at once what I was looking at. The outline of a door, I realized, heart suddenly pounding. And Dan knew it was there, he had to know. If he hadn't moved the chest, I'd never have noticed a thing.

How had he known to move the chest?

The house was very still. Were the others all still in the kitchen, or on their way up here?

I hesitated only a moment, and then I began to feel around the edges of that outlined door, prying with fingernails, pushing, prodding.

There was a funny little closet behind a door much like this at my grandma's house, under the stairs. Somehow, though, I didn't think this was a storage area.

A narrow strip of dark painted wood separated the wainscoting from the wallpaper above it. Where it, too, showed a crack, I pushed, hard.

I jumped when the section of wall swung inward, and it hadn't concealed a closet.

A narrow stairway wound downward into darkness, and there were scuff marks in the thick dust on the top steps.

Someone had used it very recently. Dan? Or the hermit from the barn? Or someone else I didn't yet know anything about?

13

If this were fiction, I thought, I'd be able to look at the footprints and identify the tread on somebody's Nikes.

No such luck. I decided, after looking at the marks in the dust, that they couldn't all have been made by one person, on one trip up or down the stairs.

From somewhere outside I heard Mickey's whoop of delight, and I turned away from the hidden doorway to cross to the window. He was in the pool, and Jill was standing on the edge of it, laughing at him. Where was Dan?

Dan. Beau. My brother's buddy who either knew too much or not enough, who might have made the tracks on the hidden stairway. Was he on the way up here right now?

I drew in a deep breath. I didn't care. Maybe it was time a few things came to a head, anyway. Time I found out what was going on, why a simple house-sitting job had turned into a nightmare.

Maybe, I thought, Sam had told his friend more than he'd told me, though it was hard to believe he'd have brought us here if he'd suspected there was any danger. If Dan caught me poking around, well, I'd demand explanations for all the things that were bothering me.

In the meantime I was going to play Nancy Drew and explore the secret stairway.

It seemed an easy decision to make, less easy to carry out. Before I lost my nerve I ran back to our room to get the flashlight, because the light switch inside the stairwell didn't work.

The hair rose with a prickling sensation on my arms as I went through the narrow opening. What if I got stuck in here? What if somebody shoved the chest back in front of the doorway while I was down inside the walls? Or I met an intruder in there?

I hesitated, three steps down. I could go and get Jill to go with me, I thought. Or Dan.

Except that I no longer trusted Dan.

Had Jill and I looked inside this room when we were exploring the house? I didn't remember. There were so many rooms, and they all looked alike with dustcovers over the furniture.

Could the chest have already been standing away from the wall, so that Dan would have noticed immediately if he'd opened the door? Or had he known where to look, and if so, how?

I'd never figure this out if I went chicken. Nancy Drew would have been all the way to the bottom by now, with all the answers.

I crossed my fingers and started downward.

The stairs wound in a rather tight spiral, and it took me long enough to reach the bottom so I had time to think a few more thoughts.

Like how Dan had plunged into searching for hidden compartments, his calm acceptance of the money in the books, his assumption that the broken chandelier wasn't a major catastrophe because it must be insured.

It would never have occurred to me to look for secret compartments, hidden stairways. The house was old, but where did you ever hear of such things outside of old-fashioned mystery novels?

I went down slowly on the circular stairs, trying to figure out where this should come out. Near the kitchen, maybe?

Was that all this was? An easy way for a servant to wait on the person in the master bedroom? No big secret after all, from the people who'd lived here?

At a small landing there was another wall switch—it didn't work, either, probably the bulbs were burned out—and there was something else. A metal handle to open another "door," which wasn't a regular door at all but another section of wall, apparently.

This door opened outward, instead of inward, and I couldn't get it open more than about two inches. There was light showing through and I put an eye to the crack and knew immediately where I was.

The stairway opened, or would if the doorway wasn't blocked by a heavy butcher-block table, into the pantry. We'd only peeked into it when we came, but I recognized the kitchen beyond.

So much for the big mystery of the secret stairway. The maid who had run up and down to Mr. Allendale's room when he was ill had simply taken this shortcut.

I couldn't remember if the big table had been in this spot before, but for sure nobody could use this doorway until it had been moved.

Someone had used the stairs recently, though. There were all those tracks in the dust, more than from a single passage through here.

The stairs continued down. After the urge to scream through the crack for help getting out of here, I remembered Nancy Drew and continued downward.

A cobweb brushed my face and a dank, musty odor hit me when I opened the door at the bottom.

How original, I thought. An ordinary basement. We ought to have realized there were basement stairs somewhere, because I remembered now that there were cellar windows, so covered with grime you couldn't see through them from the outside.

Just a basement, with a monstrous furnace and various storerooms, some locked, some standing open to reveal more junk than we'd found in the attic.

It wasn't so easy to see where the footprints went, but I didn't have to. Straight ahead of me was a short flight of steps going *up* to slanting double wooden doors.

I'd noticed them from outside, when I was looking for Sam, around behind the house, without paying them much attention. I knew Sam had secured everything about the house and I'd just assumed the doors were locked.

Now I saw that they weren't. There was a large bolt in the middle of the doors, and as I leaned to look closer I saw that the bolt had been recently oiled so it would slide easily. I tried it to make sure.

Anyone who knew the way could enter through these doors, climb the hidden stairway, and come out in the upper bedroom. They'd have access to anywhere they wanted to go in the whole house.

I slid the bolt into place, locking the doors—only was I locking someone in or out?—and fled back up the narrow stairs, past the pantry exit, and came out in Mr. Allendale's bedroom feeling as if my lungs were bursting.

Once I'd calmed down a little, which took a minute or so, I shoved hard on the chest to move it back into place.

"Hey, Lisa, you up here?"

I jumped, then moved quickly into the hallway and trotted toward the head of the stairs. "Yeah, I'm coming down," I called, "in just a minute." I needed to wash the grime of the dusty stairway off before I showed up. I hadn't decided yet who, if anybody, I was going to confide in.

Dan was obviously at the bottom of the stairs, and I didn't want to see him yet.

"Mickey says you play a little tennis. How about a match?"

I'd never felt less like tennis in my life. I knew that Sam

and Beau had played often, and I wasn't in their league. Tennis was one of the things I'd tried mainly because Marcia liked it. I've noticed that people usually like to do the things they can win.

"Uh—I don't think so, thanks. I'm lousy at it," I said, hesitating at the top of the stairs and hoping he couldn't tell from down there how grubby I was.

"So am I," Dan said, laughing. "That doesn't stop me having fun, though."

"I'll be down in a minute and we'll talk," I said, and fled to the bathroom.

It was a good thing he hadn't been any closer to me, I thought as I looked at myself in the mirror. Cobwebs in my hair, smudges of dirt on my hands and face. I cleaned up and wished I knew what to do next.

By the time I joined Dan downstairs, where we had to step carefully around the trains and the miniature village, I knew I wasn't going to tell Dan what I'd been doing for the past twenty minutes.

Because I remembered that Sam had told me Beau had a trophy for tennis, earned in high school, and that he could have made the U. Dub team if he'd wanted to.

Was he just putting himself down so it wouldn't pressure me so much? Or was there something fishy about that careless statement, too?

Too, I thought. So I was finally admitting, at least to myself, that Dan made me suspicious, though I didn't have a clue as to why he should be less than on the level with me.

I spoke before he got out more than a few words about tennis, in a tone I hoped would brook no argument. "I want to call Harborview and speak to Sam myself, if they'll let me."

I sort of expected him to throw a monkey wrench in that, too, but he didn't. "Why not? It'll make you feel better, probably," Dan agreed.

It should have made me feel better right then, but for some reason it didn't.

We decided we'd all four have to go to town, and I got more tense by the minute on the way into Arlington.

Sam was still at Harborview, we were told when we walked into the hospital. But a kind lady at the front desk gave us a phone number where she said she thought we'd be able to talk to Sam himself.

Everybody else went into the cafeteria while I stood at the pay phone in the corridor. His voice came over the line, sounding practically normal.

"Sam?"

"Lisa. How's it going?"

"How are *you* doing? Did they do that CAT scan or whatever it was?"

"They did all kinds of things. All results okay. I've still got a heck of a headache, but they say it'll go away on its own. They're shipping me back to Arlington this afternoon, and they'll probably discharge me in another day or two. You didn't call Mom and Dad, did you?"

"No. They may be mad, when they find out about you, that I didn't."

Sam laughed. "Well, you know. Parents. How you getting along with Beau?"

I hesitated. I couldn't go into everything here, on a pay phone. "He offered to play tennis with me this morning. I declined."

He laughed again. "Don't blame you. He always beats me. His sole claim to athletic fame is that tennis trophy he insists on using for a paperweight. He's the life of every party, though, so he's ahead of most of us."

"He said he'd read about old Mr. Allendale. The one who died."

"Yeah. He was a rich man, so they probably did a story on him. I guess he was kind of eccentric."

"He hid money in books," I said. I wouldn't mention the hidden stairway yet. There were more important things. "Sam, do you remember what happened to you? How you got hurt?"

There was a brief silence before Sam sighed. "Sort of. I remember falling. Not much else."

"Do you remember climbing to the loft?"

"Yeah," he said slowly. "Yeah, I looked around in the barn, didn't see anything. I climbed the ladder, at least I remember starting to climb, but not much after that. The doctor says not to push it, it'll come back to me sooner or later. I didn't fall *inside* the barn, though, did I?"

My throat was tight. "No. We found you under the loft door. You scared us pretty bad."

"Yeah. Sorry about that. Everything's okay at the house, isn't it?"

Okay? I could get hysterical, thinking about it. I didn't know what to say. I doubted he was in good enough shape yet to hear the whole story.

"You're not going to be able to go back to being caretaker right away, are you? Should I call Mr. Allendale and tell him to get someone else?"

"No, why should you do that? I've just got this headache, and it's going away. Lisa, is Beau there? Can I talk to him?"

I looked around, but there were only strangers passing in the corridor. "He's with Mickey and Jill in the cafeteria. I'm not even sure where it is."

"Oh. Well, doesn't matter. Oh, hey, they're here to get me up for a shower. How's that for progress? Yesterday I got a bath in bed. Listen, check in with the hospital regularly and see when they're going to turn me loose, okay? It could be as early as tomorrow."

"Sure," I agreed.

And then he was gone, and it was too late to ask him

111

anything else—or tell him anything—and we were stuck for at least another night at Allendale.

I hung up the phone but stood there for a moment, wondering. What would Sam remember, when his memory came back? Or would there always be a few minutes missing in what he was able to recall?

14

Dan said nothing about the hidden stairway or any of the other things that were bothering me. Like why he pretended he couldn't play tennis very well, and why he was so confident that the intruder wasn't dangerous enough to cause us to leave, and what he was prowling around the house looking for.

Several times I almost asked him how come he didn't remember Sam was a root-beer-aholic. How could they have lived in the same dorm room for a whole year without Dan noticing that the area around Sam was always littered with root-beer cans?

Sam would have asked, if he'd been in my shoes.

Marcia would have asked, and kept pushing until she got a satisfactory answer.

Why did I have to keep thinking about Marcia? She was no longer part of my life.

Nobody was part of my life. Maybe Jill would be, someday, if what was going on now finally turned out all right. If she didn't blame me for getting her into an uncomfortable situation.

Not dangerous, I told myself. Surely Dan wouldn't have encouraged us to stay if he'd thought it was dangerous.

Suddenly, as clearly as if he were here, I heard Sam saying, "For years you let Marcia do all your thinking for you; now you're letting Dan make the decisions about what's dangerous and what isn't. When are you going to grow up and think for yourself?''

He hadn't actually said that, of course. At least not the last part of it. But I *was* thinking for myself. Only so far I wasn't acting on what I was thinking. I wasn't going home where we undoubtedly belonged. I *knew* it was safe there.

Safe. Just thinking the word made me think about the alternative. Not safe. In danger.

Were we in danger? Was I letting Dan's judgment overrule my own, which could get us in real trouble, or was my gut feeling just another case of being chicken?

I had been chicken sometimes, I admitted. Not all the ways Sam had thought, like giving in to Marcia about which movie we'd watch. If it doesn't make any difference to you, why not go along with what your friend wants to do?

But what if it did make a difference? What if your friend was selfish and deprived you of the right to take your turn at choosing? Or what if a decision was really important, and you didn't have the courage to make it?

Watching Dan tapping walls and prying at every likely-looking crack around the mantelpiece and sections of paneling or pulling out desk drawers to turn them upside down and practically inside out, I kept planning what I was going to say to him.

Like, ''How come you didn't tell the rest of us that you found that hidden stairway?'' And, ''Were you the one who made all the footprints in the dust?''

When I finally spoke, from the leather sofa in the library, my voice croaked and the words didn't come out the way I'd intended.

''What made you think of looking for secret compartments?''

Dan paused in his thumping to look at me, then grinned. ''It looks like the kind of house that would have secret compartments. We already found one, so there may be more.

My . . . grandparents lived in a house like this one, and they had a secret room. Oh, just a little one, but big enough to play in. My sister—stepsister—and I hid in it once when my dad was looking for us. He was on the warpath because I'd cut Patty's hair just before they were going to have our pictures taken. My mom went into hysterics about it. Dad doesn't get mad very often, but when he does, we try to keep out of his way."

In spite of myself—his childhood reminiscences weren't what I was interested in—I asked, "What happened?"

"Oh, we hid so long they got scared about us. We missed the photographer's appointment in Seattle, but by the time we finally came out they were so glad we hadn't been kidnapped that they forgave us. After they bawled us out, of course."

Something got tight in my chest and I sat up straighter. "Is that where you grew up? Seattle?"

"In Everett, actually, north of Seattle," Dan said. He took hold of one of the carved curlicues on the trim around the fireplace and twisted, but nothing happened. "We loved coming out to Grandpa's better than being at home. There were horses, woods to run loose in, the pond to catch frogs and snakes and things that drove my mother crazy when she found them in the house."

He suddenly slammed the palm of his hand on the wall. "I know there has to be another secret hidey-hole somewhere. Let's go upstairs, look around the master bedroom again, see if there's one there."

I didn't move. My mouth was so dry I wasn't sure I could talk. "Have you ever been on the East Coast?"

"Huh? Oh, the East Coast. Sure."

"Boston?" The word felt like it was torn out of me.

"No, not Boston. New York, though. That's an exciting place. You coming with me?"

Now I not only couldn't speak, I couldn't even breathe or move.

He'd started toward the door, then stopped and looked back at me. "Lisa? Is something the matter?"

It wasn't courage I finally found. I'd just reached a stage where it was more frightening to keep still than it was to ask.

"Who are you?" I croaked, barely audible even to myself.

Startled, Dan simply stared at me.

"You're not Sam's friend Beau at all. You can't be. So who are you?"

For a few seconds he was mute. Then he licked his lips before he answered. "I told you my real name. Dan Campton."

"You let me thing you were Beau. Sam's roommate," I accused.

I was on my feet now, but I didn't walk toward him. I didn't want to get too close to him, while at the same time I wanted to hit him. Preferably with something really heavy.

"Here we come!" Mickey sang out, appearing in the doorway. "Fresh gingerbread cookies for sale!"

"Not for sale," Jill said, laughing, until she spotted us. "What's the matter?" she asked.

I told her.

For a minute we were like kids playing statue on the lawn, everybody frozen and silent.

"Who are you, then?" Mickey demanded. The plate of fragrant cookies was tipping, and Jill rescued it and put it carefully down on one corner of the big desk.

Dan looked at me, not at the others. "You took it for granted I was Beau," he said. "I never said I was. So I went along with it. I thought it was working out pretty well. What gave me away?"

"A whole string of things. Like you knew too much about this house and not enough about Sam, who was supposed to be your roommate at college. Are you the one who was hiding out in the hayloft? The one who shoved Sam out the window?''

Dan threw up his hands as if to defend himself from attack. ''Whoa! Boy, when you jump to conclusions, you go right over the cliff.''

He laughed, then reached out and took one of the cookies, warm from the oven. Nobody else made a move to touch them.

''I don't understand. What's going on?'' Jill wanted to know.

''I don't understand, either,'' I said. ''If you're really Dan Campton, who *are* you? What are you doing here? How come you went along with me taking you for Beau?''

''Hey, Jill, these are pretty good.'' He grinned, but nobody grinned back. ''Well, shoot. It seemed as good an idea as any, at the time. As far as I could tell, you kids were here legitimately. Sam had been hired as a caretaker. I expected the place would be empty. I never expected they'd hire someone to guard the place, though I should have, I guess.'' There was bitterness in his tone.

''Stop beating around the bush,'' I hissed though clenched teeth. ''Who are you, and what're you doing here?''

He sighed and sat on the edge of the desk, helping himself to another cookie. ''I'm Adam Allendale's great-grandson.''

My jaw sagged. ''His grandson? Then what are you doing sneaking around pretending to be Beau—''

''*You* took that for granted. I never said any such thing.''

''If you're an Allendale, you had more right to be here than we did. Why didn't you say so?''

Dan shook his head. ''No. If you'd called the man who hired Sam and told him my name, Uncle Stan would probably have called the police. He got a legal injunction—a court order—to keep everyone in our family off this property, so I could be arrested for being here, I guess.''

"Somebody tell me what's going on," Mickey said, scowling.

I decided I needed to sit down again. At least I no longer believed that Dan was dangerous. Jill dropped into one of the big leather chairs just inside the doorway, and with a grimace of disgust Mickey helped himself to as many of the cookies as he could hold and joined me on the couch.

I remembered something. "Did you take the photograph albums I brought down from the attic?"

"I had to. My picture was in them a hundred times or more. Pictures of me growing up, visiting my grandpa, who lived here, too. You might not have recognized me as a little kid, but I knew there was a school picture from last year in the big red album. You couldn't have missed recognizing me from that."

"Are you the one who was prowling around the cottage the night we came?" Mickey demanded. "Did you set us on fire?"

"No to both questions," Dan denied. "I suspect it was whoever's hiding in the barn, but I don't know yet who *that* is."

"I wondered," Jill murmured, and we all looked at her.

"About what?" I prompted.

"When Dan came, the way he carried in groceries and headed straight for the kitchen, without anyone telling him the way. And he seemed to know right where things were in the cupboards. And finding that secret compartment by the fireplace in the library seemed . . . a pretty lucky guess, if you didn't already know about it."

Somehow it helped to have Jill speaking out, too. Before I thought any more about it, I added, "Not to mention the hidden stairway to the basement from old Mr. Allendale's bedroom." I ignored Jill's indrawn breath. "Why didn't you tell us about finding it?"

Dan had the grace to look embarrassed. "I didn't *find* it. I already knew it was there."

Was it outrage I was feeling? I wondered. Me, chicken Lisa, Marcia's shadow and echo, afraid to strike out on my own? Talking back, expressing annoyance?

"We've been scared half to death in this place," I said. "And you made it worse."

"I'm sorry," Dan apologized.

I wasn't willing to let it go at that, though. It was kind of a heady feeling, to have finally brought a few things out in the open and to realize the earth hadn't opened up and swallowed me because of it. Jill was even watching me with what appeared to be admiration.

"I think you owe us some explanations," I said, meeting Dan's gaze.

He sighed. "Yeah. I guess I do. Maybe I didn't handle things as well as I could have, but you have to understand that you kids were a surprise to me. I didn't expect anybody to be here, and when you assumed I was somebody else, I just played along with it, thinking it would be easier. I wasn't kidding when I said if you'd told my uncle I'm here he'd have called the cops on me. And probably sued my mother for sending me here as a spy, too."

Mickey could eat and talk at the same time, when nobody stopped him. "I wish somebody'd tell me what's going on. Are you a spy? Are you looking for microfilm, or what?"

Dan laughed, but I was still kind of tense.

"Not microfilm, no. Is it okay if I begin at the beginning?"

He was asking me, so I said, "Please do."

He sat on the edge of the desk, swinging one foot, and took a deep breath. "Well, Adam Allendale was my great-grandfather. If his only son, my grandfather, hadn't died three years ago, *he* would probably have been the primary heir. He was a great guy, and he knew what he was doing right up to the end. Unfortunately,'' he added ruefully, ''that wasn't the case with Grandpa Adam.''

''He hid money in books,'' Mickey contributed eagerly.

''Among other things. Some people—including members of the family—thought he'd gone off his rocker the last few years before he died. Senile, my mom said. Not surprising, since he was ninety-two and in poor health.

''Anyway, he was always threatening to disinherit somebody if they didn't do what he wanted them to. Once he and my mom had a big fight, and he told her he'd written her out of his will. He was a generous man, in his way, but he liked being in control of things, and he didn't think women ought to be in business. My mom started a cosmetics company, which he thought was stupid in the first place, and then she wanted to expand. Sell stock in it, you know, to the public.''

He was being open, truthful, now, I thought, and I began to feel at least a willingness to forgive him. *If* he convinced me this charade of his had a reasonable purpose. I helped myself to one of Mickey's cookies.

Jill spoke unexpectedly. ''My dad says my grandmother's like that. Manipulative. He won't knuckle under to her, so they just don't see each other very often.''

''That's the word for Grandpa Adam, all right. Manipulative. Anyway, Mom first tried to explain that she was going to keep a controlling interest in her company, and then ignored him when he raged about the stock.''

Dan sighed. ''Mom's got a streak of Allendale stubbornness, too. She yelled back at him, and he said he washed his hands of her. He was taking her out of his will.''

I leaned forward. ''Is that what you're looking for? His will?''

''Oh, there's a will. Dated right after that fight. It leaves almost everything to my two uncles. But Mom thinks there was a later one. She came to visit him, here at home, just a few weeks before he died, and they had a fairly civil conversation. Expanding her company turned out to be a good idea; her profits were way up, and he always liked making a profit, so he sort of grudgingly admired that. She had the impression he was going to remake his will and put her back in it. And if he did, she feels entitled to her share of the estate.''

"Doesn't his lawyer know if there was another will?" I asked.

"Grandma Allendale told Mom she was sure he was going to change it to include her. She knows the lawyer came to the house, but he had a heart attack and died right after that, so nobody knows for sure what happened. There's no will with a later date on file, though the secretary thinks the lawyer brought papers out to the house. Ordinarily he would have taken them back to the office and had them retyped and then signed. Grandma—Grandpa Adam's daughter-in-law—thought the forms were left here and that Grandpa Adam filled in his own blanks and signed it. We don't know if anyone witnessed it—servants had been called in to do that before—but if *he* signed it, it would probably hold up in court.''

He stopped swinging his foot and stood up, and his voice was bitter. "None of the help admitted to having witnessed it, but I wouldn't have put it past Uncle Stan or Uncle Everett to bribe any signer to keep quiet so the earlier will would still be the one in effect.''

By this time I was in complete sympathy with him. "Maybe if a servant signed it, *that* person might want to find it himself. I mean, if your uncles aren't very . . . ethical . . . mightn't they *pay* someone to keep still about a later will?''

"Sure," Dan said readily. "I wouldn't put it past them. Especially if they saw the document, and it now divided the estate three ways instead of two. And ever since we found that stuff in the hayloft I've wondered if a servant who wanted to use the will for extortion was here looking for it.''

"Threatening to turn the latest will over to the authorities if your uncles didn't pay him for it so it could be destroyed,'' I said slowly, and Dan nodded.

Mickey bounced on the couch beside me. "If the will is in a secret place, how come your uncles don't know about it already? Didn't they grow up here, just like your mom?''

"They all knew about the stairway. That was put in when Grandpa Adam had a long illness, twenty years before he died. Grandma said the maids and the nurses who cared for him were worn out, running up and down the regular stairs, carrying his meals. We all knew about the compartment I pretended to 'find' beside the fireplace. I guess everybody hid things in it when they were kids. And there's another one in the desk in Grandpa Adam's room. Those were all empty, though, and I figured maybe he stuck the will in another one somewhere, one we didn't know about.''

"Your grandmother didn't know about another one?'' Jill asked, gazing around the beautiful room that certainly had plenty of possible places to hide a small object.

"Maybe she did, once. Now she's in a rest home and we're lucky if she recognizes anybody or remembers much of anything. I thought if I came here and camped out in the house—not knowing my uncles had hired a caretaker, of course—maybe I could find a newer will. My folks say we'll get by without a share of the inheritance, but . . .'' He hesitated. "Well, Mom's a pretty good businesswoman, but she trusted a guy who was a crook. He embezzled a lot of the money she got from new investors and nobody's ever caught up with him. She feels terrible that she won't be able to pay the dividends the investors have a right to this fall. There'd be plenty if she gets her share of the estate. So''—he spread his hands in a gesture of having told us everything—"I'm here without any right to be. And as soon as Sam reports that I'm here, my uncles will make sure I'm thrown out and don't have a chance to look any longer for that newer will.''

122

"It would have helped if you'd told us all that to begin with," I suggested.

Dan gave me a level look. "Would it?" he asked.

After thinking about it, I sighed. "No. Sam couldn't have let you stay, even if he believed you. Not when he's working for your uncles, who I guess are legally the heirs to the house."

Legally Dan didn't have any business being here, but ethically I figured he had more right to search for the legal will than his uncles did to prevent it being found. I stood up and made my decision. "Probably when your uncles find out what's been happening here, that Sam isn't even on the premises, only a bunch of younger kids, we'll *all* get thrown out. So we probably don't have much time left. What are we waiting for? Let's find that missing will."

15

I'd have felt better if I could have talked to Sam, whose job was on the line as soon as he could communicate with Mr. Allendale, but I hoped I knew what he'd say.

Find the will.

He wouldn't want to be a party to cheating a legitimate heir by helping the cheats suppress a legal will, I told myself. I tried not to think about the paychecks he'd be losing.

"We've already searched everywhere," Mickey complained as we stood in the library looking at thousands of potential hiding places.

"Not everywhere," I said, staring at a wall of books.

"You want us to open every one of them?" Jill asked, sounding sort of faint.

"No," Dan said immediately. "The money he stuck in the books is part of his estate, I guess, and it probably amounts to thousands of dollars, but it's the will that's important, and I doubt if he put *that* here in the books."

"Where do we look, then?" Jill asked. At least she sounded game to keep on searching, though I wouldn't have blamed her if she'd washed her hands of the whole mess. Some vacation this had turned out to be.

"Well," Dan mused, "the thing is, Grandpa wasn't completely bedridden when he supposedly had the will drawn up. He called his attorney out here, and they usually met in the study, though it's possible he wasn't strong enough that day to come downstairs. I'm sure he'd have been pretty much confined to three areas, though. The library, the study, and his bedroom.''

"That sure narrows it down," I said. "Especially if it's in a secret compartment.''

He ignored my sarcasm. "We can't rule out it being hidden here in the library. We found money in books with titles about treasures of different kinds. The will might be in a book with a *will* in the title, I suppose. It wouldn't hurt to look.''

"Or maybe," I suggested, "one with *legal* or *law* in the title. For 'legal papers' or 'law affairs' or something like that. Or just about anything else a senile old man might have thought was logical.''

How had I gotten so discouraged so quickly, when a few minutes ago I'd been determined to figure this thing out? Probably from thinking that no matter what we did, it was going to cost Sam his summer-job money.

"So what do we do?" I asked.

"One thing," Dan offered, "is that I don't think he'd have climbed on anything to hide it, which rules out anything higher than you girls can reach. Grandpa wasn't as tall as I am. And he was stiff with arthritis, so my guess is he wouldn't have gotten down too close to the floor to hide anything, either.''

If that was intended to be encouraging, I thought, it failed miserably. That only left about a million books to check out rather than two million.

"Let's split into teams," Dan said. "Jill, you and Mickey want to start here in the library? Lisa and I will finish up in Grandpa's bedroom." He shrugged. "If we can't find the will, my mom will remain officially disinherited, I guess.''

That made me a little ashamed. What was losing a summer job compared to losing a third of a fortune? On the other hand, it was Sam's job, not mine, so who was I to judge?

Dan straightened his shoulders. "Let's give it our best shot," he said, so we did.

Dan had already checked the obvious places in Mr. Allendale's bedroom, but we pulled the sheets off the furniture and I looked again while he started rolling back the rug to see if anything could have been slid beneath it.

There were photographs on the dresser, and I paused to look at them. "Are these your grandparents?"

"Yeah. Grandpa died several years ago, and Grandma's in a rest home. My great-grandma, Grandpa Adam's wife, died before I was born, so I don't even remember her. The two in the double frame are Uncle Everett and Uncle Stan, the ones who hired Sam."

I studied the pictures thoughtfully. They were handsome, prosperous men. Smiling. They didn't seem the kind of people who'd resent a sister enough to try to see her disinherited even if they had to take illegal means to do it.

"There's no picture of your mother," I said softly. "What a shame."

"It's in the nightstand drawer. At least he didn't burn her picture when he was angry with her."

I went over to the bedside and opened the drawer. The portrait was there in a heavy silver frame, and I took it out to examine it more closely. That wasn't easy to do because the glass had been broken; the lines crossed and crisscrossed the gently smiling face.

"You look a lot like her, except for your coloring," I said.

"That's what everybody says. She's pretty neat, for a mother," Dan told me.

"So's mine," I said, and thought about Mom thousands of miles away, in Europe. I could have counted on her to pick up the pieces in this mess, tell me what to do.

Only I was supposed to be trying to make decisions myself, wasn't I? Not to be Marcia's, or anybody's, shadow.

It wasn't easy, though. I wondered if I'd ever get the hang of it.

"Do you think whoever's been sleeping in the barn was coming into the house up those stairs?" I gestured toward the semihidden doorway behind the tall chest.

"I'm sure of it," Dan said, flipping up the mattress so we could see there was nothing beneath it. "That stuff dumped in the bathroom seems to me like rage that people were staying here. He probably wanted you to get scared and leave, and the same thing with the fire."

I shivered. "But he didn't care if he killed somebody. If it was up to me, I'd have gone home right then. Dan, what's going to happen if we don't find the latest will?"

He grimaced, moving a chair off the rug so he could roll up the last corner of it. "The will my uncles had will be the one that's probated. That's going on right now, actually. The money and the proceeds from selling the property, including this house, will be used to care for Grandma Allendale as long as she lives. Then the remains will be divided between Uncle Everett and Uncle Stan. My mother will be left out. And so will her stockholders."

"It's a shame she and her brothers don't get along better," I said, putting down his mother's picture. "Sam would never treat me that way."

Dan rolled up the rug, sneezing at the dust he stirred up. There was nothing else under it. "She was the youngest, and Grandpa Adam's favorite when she was little. The boys were a lot older, and they resented her even then, I think. It hurt her terribly when she quarreled with Grandpa Adam. She thought he'd come around and be reasonable, because he'd always spoiled her, but he didn't. I think it would have broken her heart if he'd died without forgiving her, if Grandma hadn't told her about the second will. At least Mom knows he didn't hate her right up to the end. In fact, he'd had her picture in his hand when he died, they thought. They found

127

it right here beside the bed, where it had slid out of his hand at the end.''

I swallowed, imagining it, and stepped a bit farther from the bed where Mr. Allendale had died. ''I wondered how the glass got broken. I was afraid maybe he'd . . . thrown it, or something, because he was mad at her.''

''No. Grandma said he'd taken to keeping it in the drawer, there, where he could reach it. He *said* he was using it to write on, you know, putting a paper on top of it for a note or something. Like he didn't want to admit he was just looking at it because he was sorry they'd quarreled and she hadn't been to see him for a while.''

There was nothing under the rug. There was nothing behind the pictures. There was nothing stuck to the bottoms of the drawers in the desk and the dresser. There was nothing in the closet except empty hangers.

I collapsed into a chair. ''We're not getting anywhere. Tell me something about your great-grandpa. What were his interests? What would he probably have done those last months he was alive?''

Dan slid down the wall to sit at my feet. His face showed discouragement, too.

''He didn't do much of anything the last few days, when he was here in bed, I guess. Wrote a few notes to people, mostly stuff that didn't make much sense. One said, 'The soup was too salty, and there was too much onion.' And there was one to Uncle Everett that bawled him out for crumpling the fender on the car. That happened when Uncle Everett was fifteen.''

Dan began to smile a little. ''When I was little, he was great. My *grandfather*, Mom's dad, was always so wrapped up in the family business that we didn't see much of him. She called him Pops, and that's what all the rest of us called him, too. It was my great-grandfather we called Grandpa. *He* was retired by the time I was about six, and he took me fishing when my dad was too busy to do it. We used to go back to the pond and watch the wildlife, catch frogs and snakes and once a baby rabbit. He had hired gardeners, but he liked to work in the dirt himself, too. He'd always let me help him plant things, and then we'd watch the little sprouts come up and turn into flowers and vegetables. He taught me to drive two years before I had driver's ed in school. He showed me how to tear apart an engine and put it back together again. He liked horses. Until just a few years ago there were always at least a dozen horses on the place, and he taught me to ride, too, when I was only about seven. Before that, he used to carry me in front of him when he rode. Just the way he did with Mom when she was that age.''

Up to now Adam Allendale had seemed simply a crotchety old man who'd disinherited a granddaughter, but his image began to change in my mind. He sounded more like my own grandpa.

It was as if Dan wasn't talking to me, anymore. He had drawn up his knees and encircled them with his arms; he was sort of staring off into space. ''The thing I remember best is the way he read to me when I was little. I didn't even want to go to school because they'd told me I'd learn to read there, and I figured if *I* could read, he wouldn't read to me any longer.''

He smiled, and I could tell he'd loved Grandpa Adam a lot, once. If *my* grandpa lived to be over ninety, would he change the way Mr. Allendale had?

''Toward the end, I was the one who read to *him*. His eyes were failing, but he enjoyed it when I read him the same books he'd read earlier to me. Stuff like *Don Quixote*, and Longfellow's *Hiawatha*. Did you ever read that? We loved it.''

His smile faded and he just looked sad. ''I suppose he got crabby because he didn't feel well, his bones ached, he couldn't do the things he'd always enjoyed doing. Several times he got so difficult Grandma just walked off and left him, refusing to deal with him, and I'd pick up a book and start reading aloud, and he'd calm down.''

Dan fell silent, then said, "I miss him, the way he was before he got sick. My dad says to remember the good times and forget bad ones, when he wasn't really responsible anymore.''

There was a lump in my throat. "It's hard to believe he'd forgive your mother, put her back into his will, and then not leave it where it would be found.''

"I don't suppose he meant to do that. He didn't expect to get as sick as he did, and then to die, that soon. He probably expected to give the new will to his lawyer when he came back, only the man died, and then so did Grandpa.''

After a moment of silence, I heaved myself out of the chair. "Well, this isn't finding the will, is it? Where else is there to look?''

"Darned if I know," Dan said, and for the first time he sounded really down. "Let's go have a cold drink and a snack. Maybe that'll inspire us to think of something useful.''

I turned to follow him out of the room, then caught a glimpse of myself in the mirror. "Why didn't you tell me I had a big streak of dirt on my face?''

"You must have backed into a dirty corner somewhere, too,'' Dan said helpfully. "There's a cobweb on the back of your shirt.''

I twisted to see, made a swipe at the offending cobweb, and made it worse.

"I'll be down in a few minutes,'' I told him. "I'll have to find a clean shirt.''

I wasn't really thinking about the clean shirt I put on after I'd washed up, only of the puzzle of a missing will and some unknown person invading the house, maybe to find it first. I turned around suddenly from the dresser and ran into Jill's suitcase that was balanced on a chair. It fell off and dumped its contents onto the floor.

I muttered under my breath and knelt to pick the stuff up. There wasn't much, because she'd put most of her things in the dresser drawers.

I picked up the pale blue top and had almost closed the lid of the suitcase on it when I stopped.

Pale blue? It was the shirt Jill had laid out the night before and hadn't put on this morning after all. And instead of being neatly folded the way it had been when she'd taken it out, it was all wadded up.

That wasn't what startled me, though. There was a hole in it, a cigarette-burn hole like the one that had made Marcia get rid of her identical shirt.

When she'd expressed her anger about the careless smoker, I'd tried to cheer her up by suggesting that she could wear it tucked in, and nobody would see the damage to it.

Marcia had given me a scornful look. "*I'd* know it was there," she said. "And what if the shirt came untucked? Then everybody would see it."

As far as I knew, she'd never worn it again.

So how come Jill had it now? She'd brought it with her, obviously intending to wear it tucked in so the hole wouldn't show, and then . . .

I'd mentioned that my friend—used-to-be friend—had a shirt like it, with a burn hole in it. Jill hadn't said a word at the time, but it had to be the same shirt. She didn't want me to know it had been Marcia's, so she'd hidden it.

How the heck had she come to have Marcia's shirt?

I stared at it, bewildered and a little disturbed. Jill didn't even *know* Marcia, did she?

I didn't think Jill was a spy for Marcia, or anything like that. Marcia had never so much as looked at the other girl, as far as I'd observed, that last couple of weeks we were in school together. And I supposed Jill had a right to be friends

131

with anybody she liked, including Marcia, but considering how Marcia and I were now practically sworn enemies, that idea made me feel funny.

I put the lid down on the suitcase, snapping it shut. One of the catches was broken and wouldn't hold, which explained why it had spilled when I knocked it over.

I went slowly downstairs, thinking up ways to approach the subject—to ask how come she had the traitorous Marcia's shirt—but I knew I wouldn't really say any of the things I thought of. It was just strange, was all.

Actually, several things about Jill weren't what I'd have expected. I didn't know anything about her family, except that she and her dad lived alone because her mother had died about a year ago. I'd never been to her house, and she'd never been to mine until I asked her to come with us to Allendale. Her dad had dropped her off and met my folks briefly. He'd been a nice man, very tired looking, but he'd smiled and talked a few minutes, and thanked us for inviting Jill to go with us.

And she herself had hardly talked at all since we'd left home. Absently, as I dodged trains and miniature buildings in the foyer and walked through the dining room where the once lovely chandelier was a mound of glittering rubble on the huge table, I mulled over what I'd learned about Jill in the past couple of days.

She'd lived in old houses where the window glass was wavy, and she recognized the smell of dead mice (and was used to disposing of them), she loved to putter around fixing fancy food and even sort of purred like a contented cat at the equipment here in the Allendale kitchen. Except for fixing Mexican foods—which Mom didn't care for, so I had to make my own or do without—I didn't spend much time in the kitchen, and Marcia had never spent any time there whatsoever. She joked about marrying some rich guy so she could have servants, because cooking was not her idea of fun.

Jill blushed easily, over things most people wouldn't have reacted to at all. She was quiet and pleasant, and so far had let me take the lead in practically everything. That, I decided, was reasonable, since she was my guest here.

Everybody else was in the kitchen, having a snack. By the time I joined them, after imagining just asking Jill point-blank about the shirt, I'd turned chicken again. I'd ask her later, I decided, when we were alone together.

No opportunity arose, though. We stayed up fairly late listening to records and built gigantic chocolate sundaes to end the evening.

I took the first shower and got into bed, planning to bring up the subject of the burned shirt when Jill joined me. Only she took so long in the shower—she seemed to be even more addicted to long showers than Sam was, and that was saying something—that I fell asleep before she got there.

I was aware of it when she finally crawled into the sleeping bag next to me, but too drowsy to want to wake up and talk. I drifted back to sleep.

Suddenly, I don't know how much later, I woke up when an engine started not too far away.

I sat up, straining to tell where it came from.

It wasn't the station wagon, I knew the sound of that motor, or Dan's silver streak, either. Sam would have said this one needed a tune-up.

It wasn't out on the road, either. It was closer than that. Maybe at the back of the house, out by the stable.

My pulses began to race as the engine roared, came closer, then gradually diminished in the distance.

Who? I wondered. Who was he? He didn't even care if we overheard him, the man who had left his meager belongings in the hayloft (who maybe had pushed Sam out of the loft?) and gone in and out of the house by the cellar door and those backstairs, deliberately frightening us so we'd go away.

Was that what he was trying to do now? Scare us away?

133

Or, the thought came as I tried to be indignant instead of scared, had he somehow accomplished what he'd come to do and found what we'd all been searching for?

16

I sat in the darkness, hearing only Jill's deep breathing; the sounds hadn't disturbed her. Would I ever be able to go back to sleep now? I wondered crossly. I thought the trespasser had *wanted* to upset us.

The whisper brought the hairs up on my bare arms.

"Lisa? You awake?"

"Dan! You heard it, too?"

"Motorcycle. It must have been hidden somewhere on the grounds or we'd have heard it come in."

I slid out of bed, shivering, though it wasn't really cold, and joined him in the dark hall.

"How could we have missed a motorcycle when we were searching for Sam?"

"I don't know. Maybe it was hidden out in the woods, though we didn't see any tracks or broken-down brush. Or maybe he walked it in so we wouldn't hear it."

"Dan, who *is* it? It gives me the creeps to think there's someone out there watching us, trying to get back inside the house!"

"I don't like it, either." Unexpectedly, Dan chuckled. "Actually, I'm a trespasser, too. My folks told me to stay away from here, and my uncles would throw me out in a minute if they had any idea I was here. They won't want anyone but themselves to find that will. If they haven't already found it and destroyed it, though I doubt they'd have hired Sam if they'd done that.''

"I'd feel better if we could just call the cops."

"Yeah, so would I. But then everybody—my uncles, my folks—would all know we're here."

We talked for a few minutes and then reluctantly went back to bed. Tomorrow, for sure, I decided, I was going to talk to Sam, tell him everything.

If we were lucky, he'd say we were going to clear out of here and let the Allendales deal with their own problems. It would be too bad about Sam's summer job, and about Dan's mother being cheated of her share of the estate, but at least we wouldn't have to worry about being murdered in our beds.

We decided over a breakfast of sausages and pancakes that there was no point in going to town before about ten o'clock. There was little chance the hospital would release Sam before that.

Dan carried his dishes to the sink and announced that he was going to take another look around and see if he could find any sign of the motorcycle we'd heard last night. "You want to come, Mick?" he invited.

Mickey shook his head. "I'm going to play with the trains until the last minute. "I've got almost everything set up. I'm going to start everything going at once. It'll be the greatest train wreck you ever saw!"

I almost choked. "You can't wreck the trains!" I protested. "They belong to somebody else!"

Before Mickey could put his indignation into words, Dan cut in. "It's okay. I used to crash them head-on and it didn't do any damage, just made them jump the tracks. They're heavy-duty, built for rough treatment. Let him crash them. If you want to start everything at once, Mick, plug in your power in that outlet beneath the lamp table. It's controlled by the wall switch at the foot of the stairs. Once you're ready, you can hit that switch and everything will take off at once. The sawmill will saw, the beacon will swing around in the airport tower, the warning bells will ring, the crossing gates will go up or down depending on where the trains are, and every engine will move.'' He glanced at me, grinning, challenging me to deny that it would be great fun.

I made a sound of disgust. ''Okay, but don't forget you have to clean up all the mess and put everything back in the attic before we leave.''

''You going to leave, too, Dan?'' Mickey asked, satisfied now that he could anticipate creating a major disaster.

''I don't know. I can't think of anywhere else to look''— Dan sighed—''but I hate to give up.''

I knew how he felt, but we *had* really tried. ''I don't understand how your mother could have been Mr. Allendale's favorite and then have cut her out of his will over something like starting a business he didn't approve of. I mean, it wasn't as if she'd done anything *wrong*.''

Dan stood up and carried his plate to the sink. ''Mom always thought—after she grew up, I mean—that it was unfortunate he'd made it so obvious that she *was* his favorite. Naturally her brothers resented it. On the other hand, they didn't climb up in his lap and give him hugs, either, so who knows? Maybe I'll take one more look around in Grandpa Adam's bedroom. I still think that's the most likely place for him to have left the will. First, though, I'm going to see if I can find where our spook had his motorcycle hidden.''

Jill and I cleaned up the rest of the breakfast things in silence, though my thoughts were furiously racing. We were alone now, and this was as good a time as any to ask Jill about the things that were bothering me. Only I couldn't quite think of a way to start.

Jill finally provided me with enough of an opening to begin when she put the last plate in the dishwasher and closed the door and latched it.

137

"You act as if you actually *enjoy* working in the kitchen," I said.

"I do." Jill looked around at the gleaming appliances and rows of cabinets and counters. "This is a beautiful kitchen."

"Yeah, it's nice," I agreed. "Is it the dishwasher? Don't you have one at home?"

Then it happened again: Her face flamed bright pink. "Not now," she said. "We did have one, before Mom died."

"Where do you live, anyway? Marcia and I were in and out of each other's houses all our lives. I feel sort of funny that I've never even found out where you live."

I wasn't prepared for her reaction. For a matter of seconds her face was absolutely crimson. Then all the color drained away and she was so pale I was alarmed.

"Jill? What's the matter?"

She stared at me, eyes wide and scared looking. It made me kind of scared, too.

"What's going on? Is something wrong?" I asked.

Her throat worked as if she wanted to speak, but couldn't. On impulse, I put out a hand to touch her hand and found that it was icy.

"Jill, are you okay?" It was a stupid question, because obviously she was very upset, though I couldn't imagine why. "Is it something to do with Marcia?"

She did manage to speak, then, though her voice quavered. "Marcia?" she echoed. "Why should it have anything to do with Marcia?"

I was getting more confused by the moment. "Well, I only thought—maybe you and Marcia were friends, but you didn't say anything because you knew how she'd treated me—" I could tell from her face I was on the wrong track, but I didn't have a clue as to what the *right* track was.

She shook her head. "I told you, I don't even know Marcia. I've never spoken to her."

"But you've got her shirt," I blurted. "The one somebody

burned with a cigarette. I thought—'' I stopped, because I didn't really know what I thought.

Jill went red and then pale again, and sank onto a chair as if her legs were shaking. Mine were beginning to, and I sat down, too, across the table from her.

She looked so awful I felt I had to apologize, though I wasn't quite sure why. ''I didn't mean to snoop,'' I said. ''I accidentally knocked your suitcase off the chair, and it spilled, and I saw the shirt. I knew it was the same one because of the burn hole. If you didn't get it from Marcia—''

She didn't look at me but down at her hands, locked together so hard on the tabletop that her knuckles were white. ''I got it at a thrift shop.''

''A thrift shop?'' I echoed, still trying to sort things out. ''Oh. I guess I should have thought of that. Marcia's mom does donate things to a thrift shop sometimes. But what's the big deal? What's wrong with that?''

Jill did look at me, then, and to my horror there were tears in her eyes. ''We get all our clothes at thrift shops.''

''And you're embarrassed about it?'' I asked. ''My grandma often gets things at thrift shops. It's sort of a hobby with her, going through stuff there.''

One tear spilled over and ran down Jill's cheek, but she was still looking at me. ''It's different when . . . you *have* to go there.''

''Have to? You mean . . . you can't afford to buy stuff in a regular store?''

She swallowed. ''I guess I should have told you.''

''Told me what? That you're . . . poor?'' It was awkward to say the word, because I suddenly was beginning to get some uneasy feelings about just how poor Jill and her dad were. ''You told me your dad was looking for another job, so we couldn't call him and ask his advice about staying here—''

Jill suddenly appeared almost defiant, though her mouth

139

trembled. "We couldn't call him because we don't have a telephone. We don't even have a house to put a telephone in."

I ran that past my mind, which seemed to be getting sort of numb, for a second time. "You don't have a house," I repeated, hoping if I said it aloud it would begin to make sense.

Jill turned and looked out the window to where we could see the boys on the edge of the woods. "We live in a tent in the campground east of town."

When I didn't say anything—I was still sorting all of this out—she swallowed hard again and added, "Until we got the tent last month, we lived through most of the winter in our car."

It all clicked then. I'd seen a little bit about it on television: homeless people, living on the streets. Not just bums or burned-out druggies, but whole families without homes.

I hadn't *really* thought much about it, though. I mean, *I* had never met anyone who lived on the street or in their car. It was something that happened to people you didn't know.

"But your dad has a job—I know you said it didn't pay very well, but—" I didn't know what to say.

Jill continued to stare out the window so she wouldn't have to look at me. "Mom was sick for a long time. Our insurance ran out, and then we lost our house because we couldn't make the payments on it and take care of her hospital bills, too. We tried living with my grandparents, but—"

Her hands came apart and made helpless fluttering motions. "We tried renting, mostly crummy old apartments with mice and leaky roofs and—" She stopped, then started over. "The last place was full of drug dealers. We were afraid to be there, and we moved into the car. Just until we could find a decent place, you know? Only all the landlords wanted the first and last months' rent, and a cleaning deposit, and Daddy was only working part of the time—"

She sounded so helpless, so sad, that I felt tears in my own eyes. "So you just stayed in the car. With no kitchen, no bathroom—" When the reality of that hit me, I stopped.

Jill's smile was crooked. "Yes, no bathroom. Do you know how many places lock up their public rest rooms these days? We had trouble finding a place to wash up or anything, and they don't let you stay in the state and county parks for more than two weeks at a time. So we moved around from one to the other, every two weeks. At least in the parks they usually had rest rooms and showers and laundry rooms. When the weather was decent we could cook a little on the barbecues. The rest of the time we just"—she had trouble with her throat again—"ate out of jars or cans, stuff we could eat cold, that didn't have to be refrigerated."

It practically made my head swim to imagine how awful it must have been. "You could have told me," I said softly, though admittedly it was making me feel sort of sick to hear it now.

Jill ran her tongue over her lips to moisten them. "Where I went to school last, some of the kids found out. They weren't . . . nice. They said . . . things."

I could imagine that, too, and there were probably a lot of horrors that hadn't yet occurred to me.

Now it was my own throat closing up that made talking difficult. "It'll get better," I said, wondering if that were true. "When your dad gets a better job."

Jill nodded slowly. "That's what we've been saying. For almost a year now."

A year. A year, living in a car, and now in a tent. My throat ached, and I didn't know what to say.

"We're trying to save enough money to get into an apartment," Jill said. "But things keep happening, so we have to spend what we've saved. Like the car breaks down and has to be fixed or Daddy can't even go to work. Or one of us gets hurt and needs a doctor. Things like that."

Now I was getting a cramp in my stomach, because my imagination was starting to run wild. About things like where did you keep your clothes when you were living in a tent, or your groceries, or anything else? How did you brush your teeth or wash your hair when you didn't have running water? No wonder she took such long showers now!

"Where did *you* go when your dad took the car to work?" I blurted.

Her voice was very soft. "In the parks, in nice weather, I just kept my sandwiches and a book to read on one of the picnic tables. Sometimes, when the weather wasn't so good, or after school in the winter, I spent my time in the public library."

She gave me a little half smile that made me want to cry. "Actually, libraries are rather nice. Besides all the books, they're warm and they have bathrooms where you can clean up."

My eyes were stinging. "And I was feeling sorry for myself when we came because somebody I trusted lied and made people think I swiped a stupid old sheet of test answers." It didn't seem nearly as big a problem when compared to Jill's having to live in a car for nearly a year. "No wonder you didn't talk very much! You could have told me, though."

Jill gulped. "I wanted to, Lisa. I really did. I hated . . . pretending to be just . . . normal. But some of the kids before, they'd made remarks, made fun of me . . . and I thought maybe you wouldn't have to know until after we'd . . . become friends."

"We are friends," I assured her. "After what you've been going through, I suppose all of this seems sort of . . . unimportant. Searching for a will that will give more money to people who obviously already have quite a bit." I thought of Dan's silver streak and what he'd told me of his family.

Jill shook her head. "No. Not unimportant. Just kind

of . . . detached, from my own life. It's been nice to have something else to think about. And I do appreciate your inviting me, Lisa.''

My own words were just as earnest. ''I'm glad you came. I had trouble working up to telling you that some people think I'm a thief and a cheat, too.''

''I knew you weren't,'' Jill told me. For a moment we stared at each other, both uncomfortable at feeling so much emotion, and not knowing quite what to do next.

''It's pretty here,'' Jill said, glancing around the big sunny kitchen. ''It's been nice, living in a house again.''

Mom says when you don't know what to say, sometimes it helps to give somebody a hug. I couldn't quite do that, but I reached across the table and took her hand. Jill's closed around mine in a hard squeeze, and we just sat there without talking until we heard the boys coming in.

''He kept the cycle back in the woods,'' Dan said immediately, not noticing that anything was wrong with us. ''He was careful not to make a trail in from the driveway, but once we got off the road we could see where he'd tramped down the grass and broken off a few bushes. And the motorcycle had leaked oil. But it's gone now.''

I could hardly think about that; I was too churned up about Jill and her dad, and I didn't know a thing anybody could do for them. When my own parents came home, I'd tell them and see if they had any ideas, though I couldn't guess what they'd be.

Dan opened the refrigerator and got out a can of pop. ''Well, I guess I might as well give up and put everything back where it was in Grandpa's bedroom. No sense making my uncles mad by leaving it so they can tell I was here.''

In a way I was grateful that he hadn't noticed that Jill and I were so subdued. I wasn't up to explaining why, and I didn't think she was, either.

''I'll help,'' I said, and Jill got up, too.

We left Mickey eagerly setting up his catastrophe scene and went upstairs. It was a shame to let Dan's rotten uncles get away with cheating his mother, but what else could we do? I stared again at the photograph of Dan's mother. A nice lady, I thought. How hurt she must be at what had happened. I wasn't really thinking about her, though. I was thinking about Jill and her dad, and losing her mother and then their home. My eyes blurred for a moment, and I blinked the moisture away.

Well, it was just about over. I couldn't believe Sam would decide to stay on here any longer, knowing the truth about his employers. As soon as he got out of the hospital, we'd go home, and Dan's mom would never be sure that her grandfather had put her back into his will, and her stockholders would do without their dividends. And Jill would return to living in a tent that had to be moved every two weeks.

I picked up the portrait of Mrs. Campton to replace it in the drawer where I'd found it and felt the broken glass shift inside the frame. "I'm going to take the pieces out so they don't gouge into the picture and ruin it," I said, and turned it over to work the backing free.

There were several layers of cardboard, and even before I spotted a white layer in between the darker ones my heart began to beat a little faster.

Mr. Allendale had been holding it and dropped it as the life went out of his body, Dan had said. "Or was he just reaching for it and died before he got it out of the drawer?"

"What?" Dan turned to look at me.

"What if he wanted to look at her picture, at the last minute? Or maybe he wanted to write one last message to someone—your mother, maybe? Dan, there's something here, between . . ."

My voice died away as I separated the cardboard and then I forgot to breathe for a moment. Dan and Jill were beside me when I picked it up.

144

On the plain white envelope, written in a tremulous hand, it said *Last Will and Testament of Adam William Allendale*.

"Maybe," I speculated further, handing it over, "he was trying to reach the will, where he'd hidden it until his lawyer could come—only why would he feel he needed to hide it?"

"He hid all kinds of things," Dan reminded me. "Like money in books. And maybe after he'd finished it he didn't want anyone else to read it before he handed it over to the lawyer. You could be right, Lisa. He could have realized that he was dying and tried to get it out so it would be found—I guess we'll never know. But we were right about there being another will."

We were all grinning like little kids on Christmas morning. Dan ripped open the envelope and shoved the document it contained out where we could see it. "Look at the date. Just a few days before he died. This one will overrule the one my uncles have."

"Let's go down and tell Mickey," I said. "And then go to town and call your mom, and *then* go see if they're letting Sam out of the hospital."

We practically ran for the stairs. Halfway down I yelled at my little brother. "We found it, Mick! Look!"

And then the unfamiliar voice spoke from the doorway of the living room at the far side of the entry hall.

"All right. Bring it down, and just hand it over to me."

I nearly fell and grabbed for the banister as Jill careened into me.

I knew immediately that he was the man who had invaded the house and had been hiding out in the stable. That was startling enough.

But what suddenly turned my euphoria of a moment ago to terror was the gun the stranger held in his hand, pointed right at the three of us on the stairs.

17

My momentum carried me almost to the foot of the stairs before I could stop. Jill and Dan were right behind me, and I heard Jill suck in a sharp breath.

The man with the gun was about fifty years old, a slight and grizzled individual who wouldn't have scared me at all if it hadn't been for the revolver.

"Well, Heichmann," Dan said. He sounded surprisingly cool under the circumstances. "I might have known if any of the servants were crooks, it would be you. Grandpa made a mistake when he gave you a second chance after you stole from him the first time."

He brought a hand down on my shoulder—was it to steady me or to warn me? I wondered wildly, clinging to the banister.

"Mr. Heichmann," Dan said for our benefit, "was a groom here once, so he knows his way around. He's good with horses, but he's not particularly honest. How'd you get inside the house?"

For a moment the man stared at Dan with contempt. "You thought you was smart, locking the cellar door, didn't you? Well, it meant I had to go home in town and get my lock-picking tools, but that side door off the dining room is a cinch for anybody really wants to get in."

I felt as if a giant hand was squeezing my chest so it was

hard to breathe. It was even heavier than the hand still resting on my shoulder.

The man called Heichmann licked his lips, holding that ugly looking gun pointing right at me. Or was it pointing at Dan?

"If I understood you right, you found the will. Hand it over."

Out of the corner of my eye I could see Dan's free hand holding the white envelope. He slapped it casually against his thigh.

"How'd you know there was another one?" Dan asked, and I marveled that he didn't sound the way I felt: terrified.

The former groom's mouth twisted in a grin. "I was called in to sign it as one of the witnesses, actually. There being nobody else available at the time. The other one was that Marris fellow, and he's dead. So who's to say there ever was another will than the one your uncles have? Except for me, of course."

"And you want to use it to blackmail them," Dan speculated. "If they pay you, you won't hand this over to the authorities, and the will they have will stand up in court."

Heichmann showed uneven, discolored teeth in a sneer. Although we were yards apart, I was sure I could smell the tobacco on him, and it made me queasy.

"You always was a smart-mouth brat. You got it all figured out. Well, why not? It ought to be worth plenty to Everett and Stan not to have that will ever turn up. So hand it over."

"And what happens to us?" Dan asked. He sounded the same, but I could feel the increased tension in the pressure of his hand.

Something shifted in Heichmann's face. He did not want to reveal his thoughts, I thought, and felt my pulse begin to race.

"Nothing," the man said. "No way you can prove there was another will, only your word against mine. I'll 'sell' it

147

to Everett and Stan, take my money and go. They can burn it up or do whatever they want with it. Without it, your say-so won't hold up in court."

It wasn't necessarily true, I thought. Even if Dan's fingers hadn't cut sharply into my shoulder, I'd have known it. The three of us, Dan and Jill and I, hadn't read the will, but we'd seen the date on it, had read what the envelope contained. It would be the word of all three of us against his.

I didn't know what a judge would decide in a case like this, if the legal will had been deliberately destroyed, but I didn't think Dan's uncles would want to risk it.

Heichmann knew that, too. He knew the will we had just found would not be worth nearly as much to him as he'd hoped, not if three of us—or four, counting Mickey—were aware of its existence.

"I never liked you very well," Dan said now, "but I didn't take you for a killer, Heichmann."

Beyond the gunman, I saw Mickey's face. His mouth had fallen open and he was clearly terrified.

Heichmann hadn't paid any attention to my little brother. "I told you nothing would happen to you. Give me the envelope."

"Not hardly," Dan said.

"Hey. I don't want to shoot anybody. But I've been looking all over this confounded place, trying to find where the old man put that will. I tried to scare you off, nice and easy, but you were too stubborn to go. Now, if you don't hand over that envelope, I'm going to have to get nasty. Like maybe I'll shoot *her* first."

I flinched, because I no longer questioned where that gun was aimed. Right at my middle.

Another fire like the one in the gatekeeper's cottage would conceal any evidence, I thought, wondering how long I could keep on breathing when it hurt so much. Well, no doubt

148

they'd find what was left of our bodies, but we sure wouldn't be able to testify, and nobody'd know about the will.

"Give it to me," Heichmann insisted.

I jerked when Dan suddenly complied. Only he didn't throw the envelope far enough to land at Heichmann's feet. Instead it fell in the midst of Mickey's village, among the trains and tracks and tiny buildings.

Heichmann swore, and for a minute I thought he'd squeeze that trigger.

But the will was there in plain sight, and closer to Heichmann than to us. Almost within his reach.

The former groom stepped forward, cursing again because there was hardly room between the tracks for him to put his foot down.

I don't know where the idea came from. Between hearing Jill's story and now standing here with a gun trained on me, it was a miracle I could think at all, but for once I didn't waste any time evaluating the risk.

I took one more step downward and reached for the wall switch at the bottom of the stairs.

The effect, as Dan said later, was electrifying. Literally.

Mickey had everything set up for his grand catastrophe. At the touch of the switch, it went into action.

The trains moved in all directions, whistling and chuffing. Lights flashed, bells rang, the saw on the sawmill began to move.

Heichmann was in midstep when the miniature village snapped into motion. He brought a foot down on what a moment before had been a section of track, only now there was a speeding train on it. The sturdy engine smashed into the side of his foot, hard. It threw the man off balance, twisting an ankle so he yelped with the pain of it. He crashed down backward, landing on a second tiny freight train and smashing several houses into splinters.

The hand holding the gun waved wildly, then wound up aiming at the ceiling for a matter of seconds.

It was enough. Dan bounded past me, knocking me against the wall, and kicked at the wrist holding the gun. Heichmann yelped again and lost the revolver, which went skidding between an eight-inch skyscraper and a fire station with small-scale red trucks peeking out of it.

Dan leaped a section of track and a speeding train that moments later crashed into the sprawled Heichmann. They both scrambled for the gun, and it was Dan who grabbed it.

He and Heichmann were both breathing heavily, but with the revolver now pointed at *him*, the former groom didn't get up.

Dan spoke to Mickey without looking at him, digging into his pocket for keys with his free hand. "Here, Mick, find the one for the trunk and bring in the rope you'll find in it. No, don't move, Heichmann. Just stay there."

He looked a little pale, but he grinned at Jill and me. "I'm no hotshot at tennis, but my karate lessons just paid off."

Heichmann glared at us, shifting position to get off the steeple of the tiny white church. Even from where I was I could see that his ankle was swelling rapidly, and there was blood on one palm where he'd landed on something sharp. Hatred was written on his face, but he did what Dan said. He stayed put when Mickey brought the rope, and we tied him up.

And that was really the end of our adventure at Allendale. We hauled Heichmann into town—nervously, to be sure, but we made it—to the Sheriff's Department. We got Sam out of the hospital and over Big Macs and Cokes gave him sort of an incoherent (with four of us talking at once) account of what had happened that he didn't know about.

He was sorry about losing his summer job, but he said he'd just go home and study and see if Mom and Dad wouldn't cosign for a loan to get him back in school.

Dan called his mom and told her he'd found the will and would take it to her lawyers right away. I guess she cried a little, not so much because of the money she'd get but because it proved her grandpa had forgiven her and really loved her, after all.

So we went home, to fat Mrs. Gottman and her constant conversation and soap operas, to wait for Mom and Dad to return from Europe. Sam and I agreed, with no discussion, that none of what had happened was anything to try to relate over the international phone lines.

Four days later Beau showed up. He was every bit as handsome as Sam had described, and he really laid on the charm. I mean, he treated both Jill and me as if he thought we were charming, too. The kind of thing that makes any girl feel glad she's a girl. Only after he'd been around for a few days, I decided he wasn't really as genuine and *nice* as Dan was.

Jill stayed with us, in my room, and we talked about a lot of things. Not quite the same way Marcia and I had done, but we each knew the worst about the other, and I knew we were going to be friends as long as she and her dad lived in Granite Falls.

"I feel awful about her going home to a tent," I told Mom later. "It was fun staying in a tent when we went camping in the Cascades, but it would be a lot different having to live in one."

"Yes, it would," Mom agreed.

"And the worst thing is that I don't know anything to do to help her," I said earnestly. "What can a kid do about anything serious like a friend not having a place to live?"

"The same as you'd do for any problem a friend has," Mom said thoughtfully. "Like having a younger sister who's retarded, or having to walk with leg braces, or not being able to walk at all, or having terrible burn scars that make people stare."

I didn't get it. "But I couldn't do anything about any of those things!" I protested.

Mom smiled very gently. "Not to change them, no. But to make your friend feel better, you can understand that they can't help their circumstances. You can imagine how it would feel, to have no home or a handicap that can't be cured."

"Like having people think you're a cheat and a thief," I said hollowly.

Mom smiled a little. "Anything you can't help, that hurts a person. In that case, kindness helps."

Kindness. That didn't seem like very much. It wouldn't change the circumstances. But I could see, when I went to visit Jill at the campground and we went swimming in the Stillaguamish River and changed clothes in the tent, that she was really glad I'd come, so maybe Mom was right.

And when I met some of the kids at the Tom Thumb Grocery, I was relieved when they said, "Hi, Lisa, you been away on vacation?" just the way they'd always greeted me. I was grateful. Maybe everybody *hadn't* believed I'd stolen the test answer sheet.

And when Dan came out in the silver streak to pick up Sam and Mickey and Jill and me to drive into Seattle Center for the dinosaur exhibit (for Mickey) and dinner at the Space Needle and a ball game afterward (for the rest of us) I was able to tell him about being accused of theft and cheating, and he understood how I felt.

We were in Konnerup's, picking up some junk food to last us until we got to the Center, when I came around the end of an aisle and ran smack into Marcia.

She looked startled, then took in Dan's lean good looks and flashed us that famous brilliant smile that knocked everybody dead. At least it had until now.

"Oh, hi, Lisa!" She really turned on the charm when she looked at Dan. "I'm Lisa's friend Marcia," she gushed.

Dan nodded without returning her smile. "I've heard about you," he said coolly. "Excuse us, we're in a hurry."

He touched my elbow to get me moving and we walked away toward the checkout counter, leaving Marcia with her mouth hanging open. It was probably the first time any guy had ever turned his back on her.

The cashier was Jenny Childress, who'd been in my grade all through school since kindergarten. She slid an admiring glance at Dan, too, and I had a hunch it would be all over Granite Falls within minutes that I'd been seen with a really good-looking boy who drove a terrific car.

Marcia was still staring when we passed her and went out the door without speaking to her.

"Be kind," Mom had said. In Marcia's case, I decided I'd have to think about it.

Jill was watching from the car. Her face was alight with anticipation of the outing as she reached out to take our bag of chips. "Oh, good, taco and barbecue," she said. "I made some Cajun dip. Do you think that'll be too many different flavors?"

"Perfect," Dan and I said together, and we all laughed.

Be kind, Mom had said. It seemed so little to do. But maybe, sometimes, it's enough.

About the Author

Willo Davis Roberts is the author of over sixty books, most of them mystery, suspense, medical background, and historical novels. She has four grown children, two sons and two daughters, who also write, and four grandchildren. She lives in Washington state with her husband, David, also a writer/photographer. Her previous book for Fawcett was the very successful *Babysitting Is A Dangerous Job*.